THE SMURF
APPRENTICE

Peyo

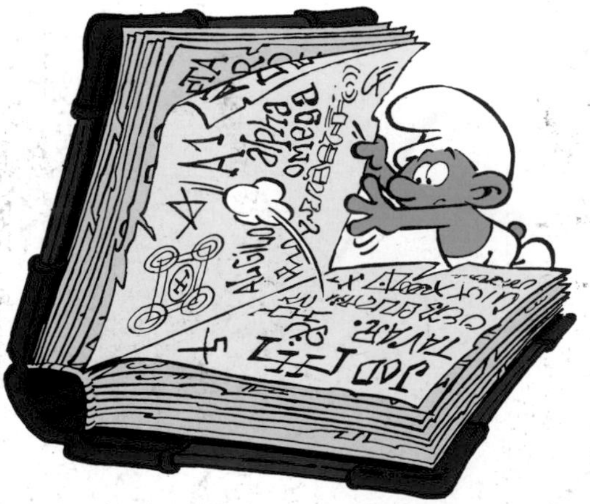
alpha
omega

THE SMURF APPRENTICE

I heat it...
And presto! It's ready!
I pour it on this seed and...
BOOM

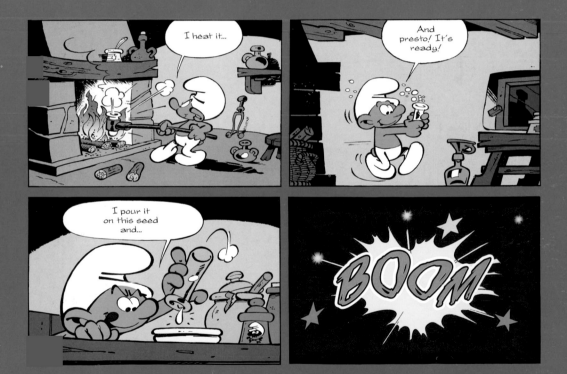

A SMURFS GRAPHIC NOVEL BY Peyo

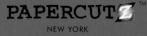

PAPERCUTZ™
NEW YORK

SMURFS GRAPHIC NOVELS AVAILABLE FROM **PAPERCUTZ** ™

1. **THE PURPLE SMURFS**
2. **THE SMURFS AND THE MAGIC FLUTE**
3. **THE SMURF KING**
4. **THE SMURFETTE**
5. **THE SMURFS AND THE EGG**
6. **THE SMURFS AND THE HOWLIBIRD**
7. **THE ASTROSMURF**
8. **THE SMURF APPRENTICE**

COMING SOON:

9. **GARGAMEL AND THE SMURFS**
10. **THE RETURN OF THE SMURFETTE**
11. **THE SMURF OLYMPICS**

The Smurfs graphic novels are available in paperback for $5.99 each and in hardcover for $10.99 each at booksellers everywhere.

Or order through us. Please add $4.00 for postage and handling for the first book, add $1.00 for each additional book. Please make check payable to NBM Publishing. Send to: PAPERCUTZ, 40 Exchange Place, Suite 1308, New York, NY 10005 (1-800-886-1223).

WWW.PAPERCUTZ.COM

THE SMURF APPRENTICE

SMURF™ © Peyo - 2011 - Licensed through Lafig Belgium -
English translation Copyright © 2011 by Papercutz.
All rights reserved.

"The Apprentice Smurf"
BY PEYO

"Smurf Traps"
BY PEYO AND GOS

"The Smurfs and the Mole"
BY PEYO

Joe Johnson, SMURFLATIONS
Adam Grano, SMURFIC DESIGN
Janice Chiang, LETTERING SMURFETTE
Matt. Murray, SMURF CONSULTANT
Michael Petranek, ASSOCIATE SMURF
Jim Salicrup, SMURF-IN-CHIEF

PAPERBACK EDITION ISBN: 978-1-59707-279-3
HARDCOVER EDITION ISBN: 978-1-59707-280-9

PRINTED IN CHINA SEPTEMBER 2011 BY WKT CO. LTD.
3/F PHASE I LEADER INDUSTRIAL CENTRE
188 TEXACO ROAD, TSEUN WAN, N.T., HONG KONG

DISTRIBUTED BY MACMILLAN.
FIRST PAPERCUTZ PRINTING

THE APPRENTICE SMURF

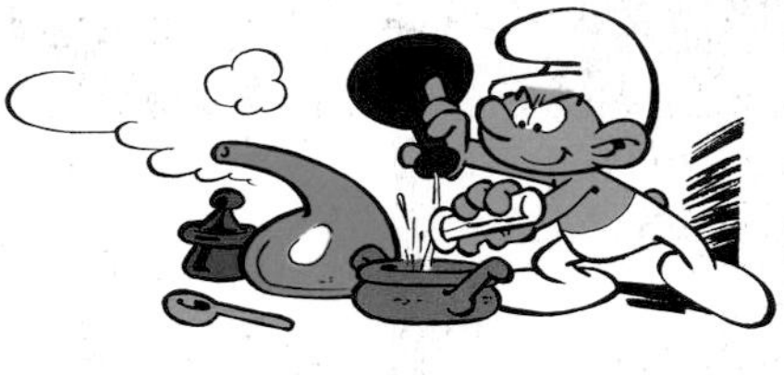

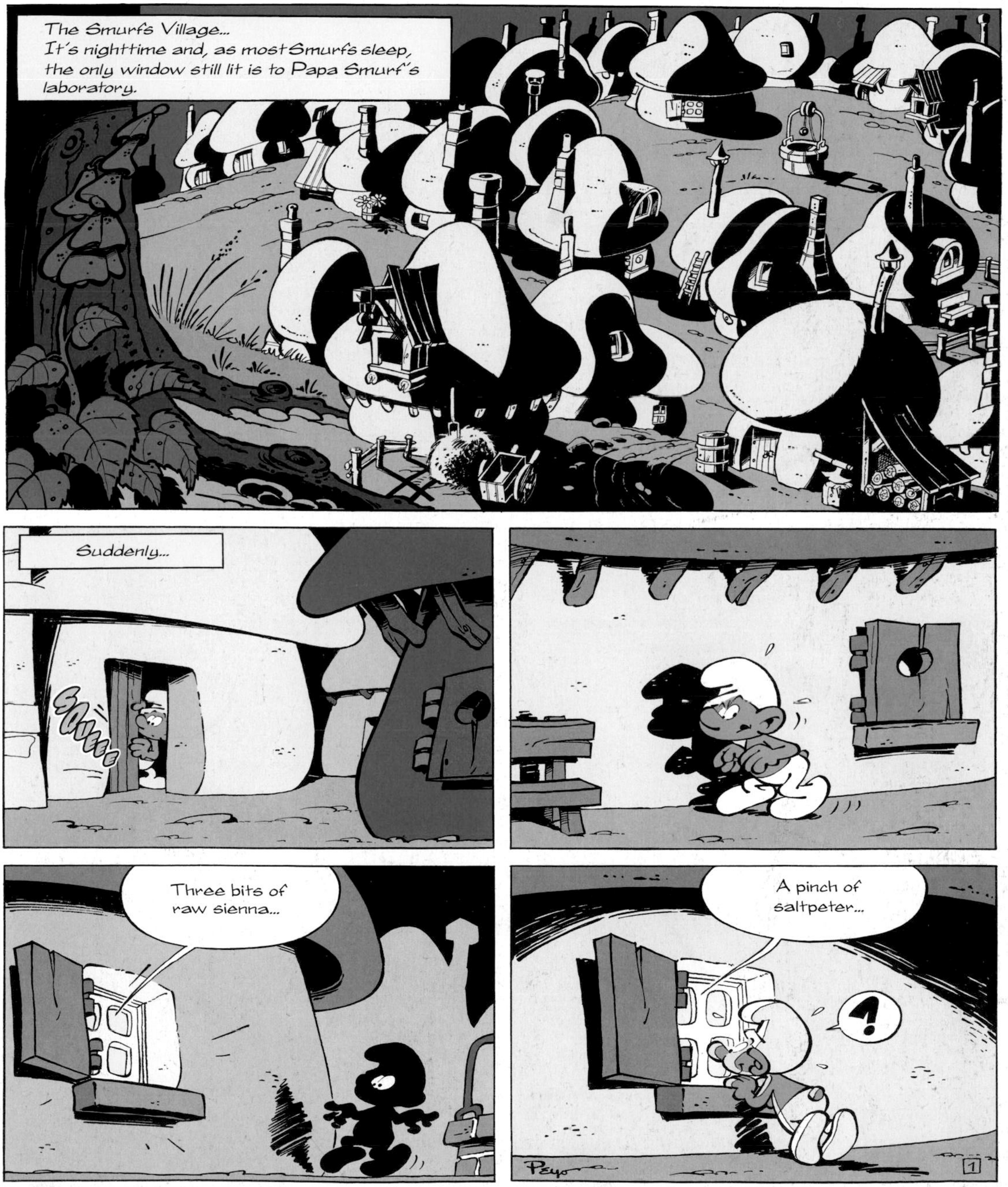

The Smurfs Village...
It's nighttime and, as most Smurfs sleep, the only window still lit is to Papa Smurf's laboratory.
Suddenly...
Three bits of raw sienna...
A pinch of saltpeter...
?
Peyo
1

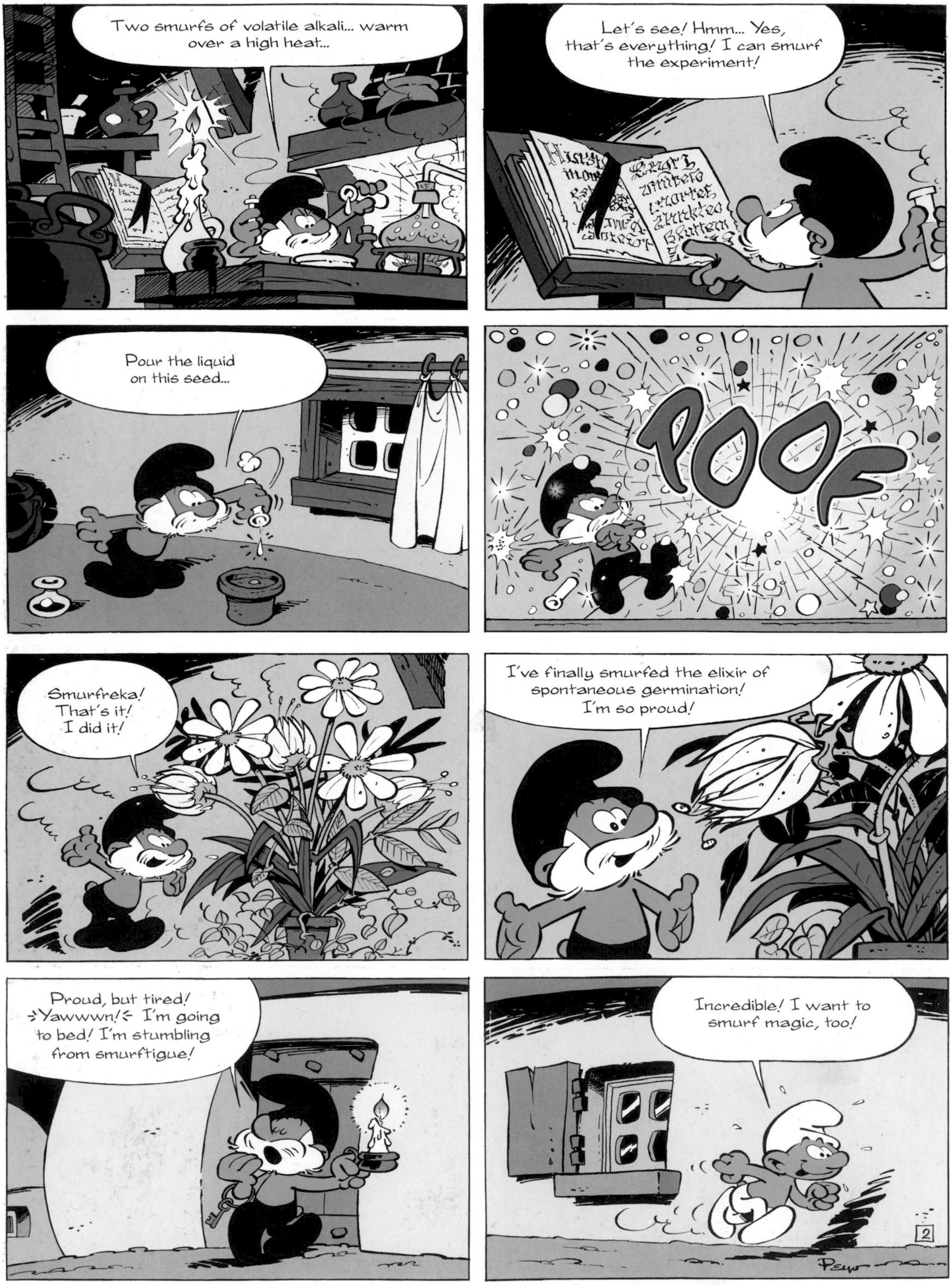
Two smurfs of volatile alkali... warm over a high heat...
Let's see! Hmm... Yes, that's everything! I can smurf the experiment!
Pour the liquid on this seed...
POOF
Smurfreka! That's it! I did it!
I've finally smurfed the elixir of spontaneous germination! I'm so proud!
Proud, but tired! ⇾Yawwwn!⇽ I'm going to bed! I'm stumbling from smurftigue!
Incredible! I want to smurf magic, too!
2

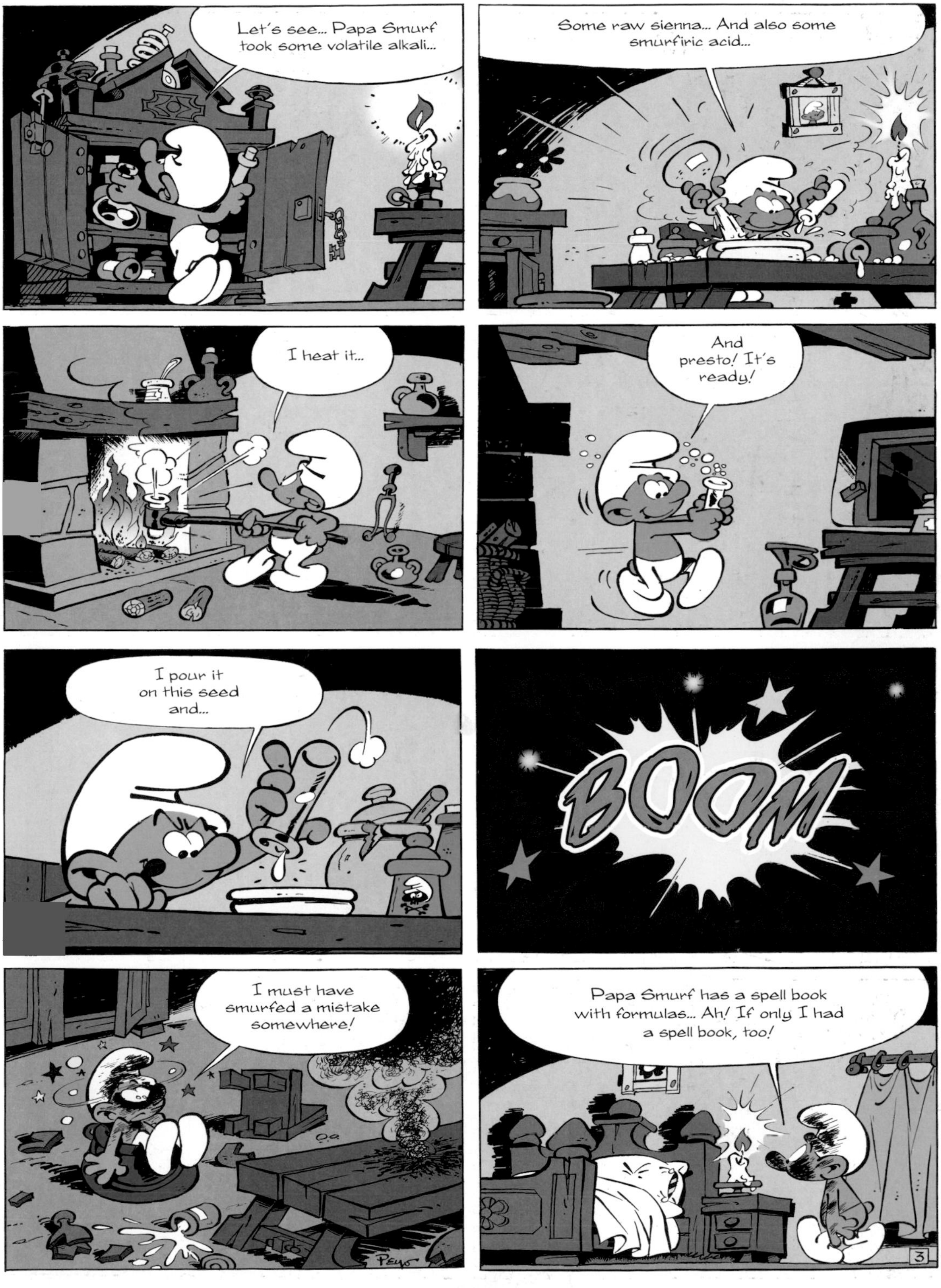
Let's see... Papa Smurf took some volatile alkali...
Some raw sienna... And also some smurfiric acid...
I heat it...
And presto! It's ready!
I pour it on this seed and...
BOOM
I must have smurfed a mistake somewhere!
Papa Smurf has a spell book with formulas... Ah! If only I had a spell book, too!

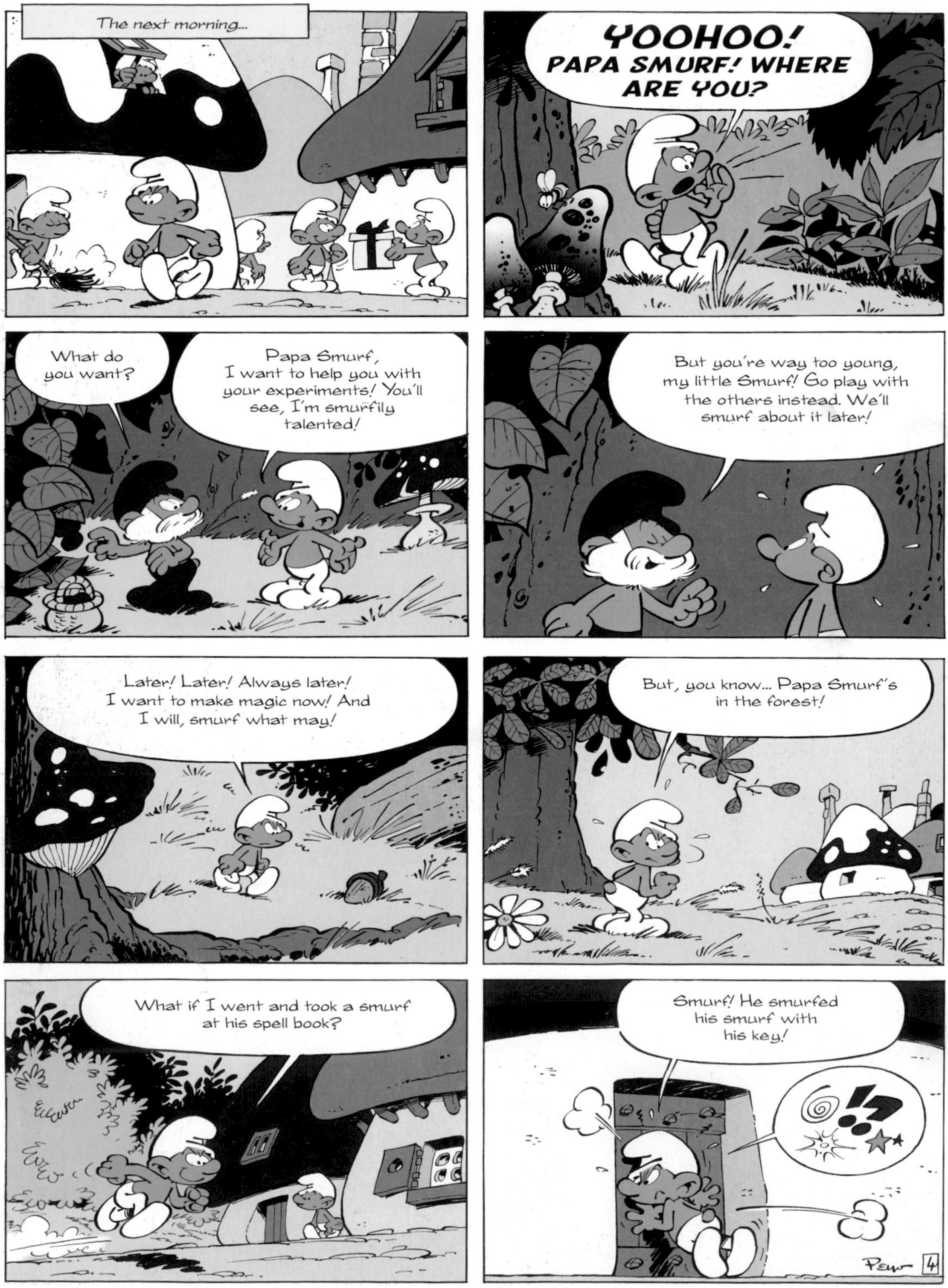

The next morning...
YOOHOO! PAPA SMURF! WHERE ARE YOU?
What do you want?
Papa Smurf, I want to help you with your experiments! You'll see, I'm smurfily talented!
But you're way too young, my little Smurf! Go play with the others instead. We'll smurf about it later!
Later! Later! Always later! I want to make magic now! And I will, smurf what may!
But, you know... Papa Smurf's in the forest!
What if I went and took a smurf at his spell book?
Smurf! He smurfed his smurf with his key!
4

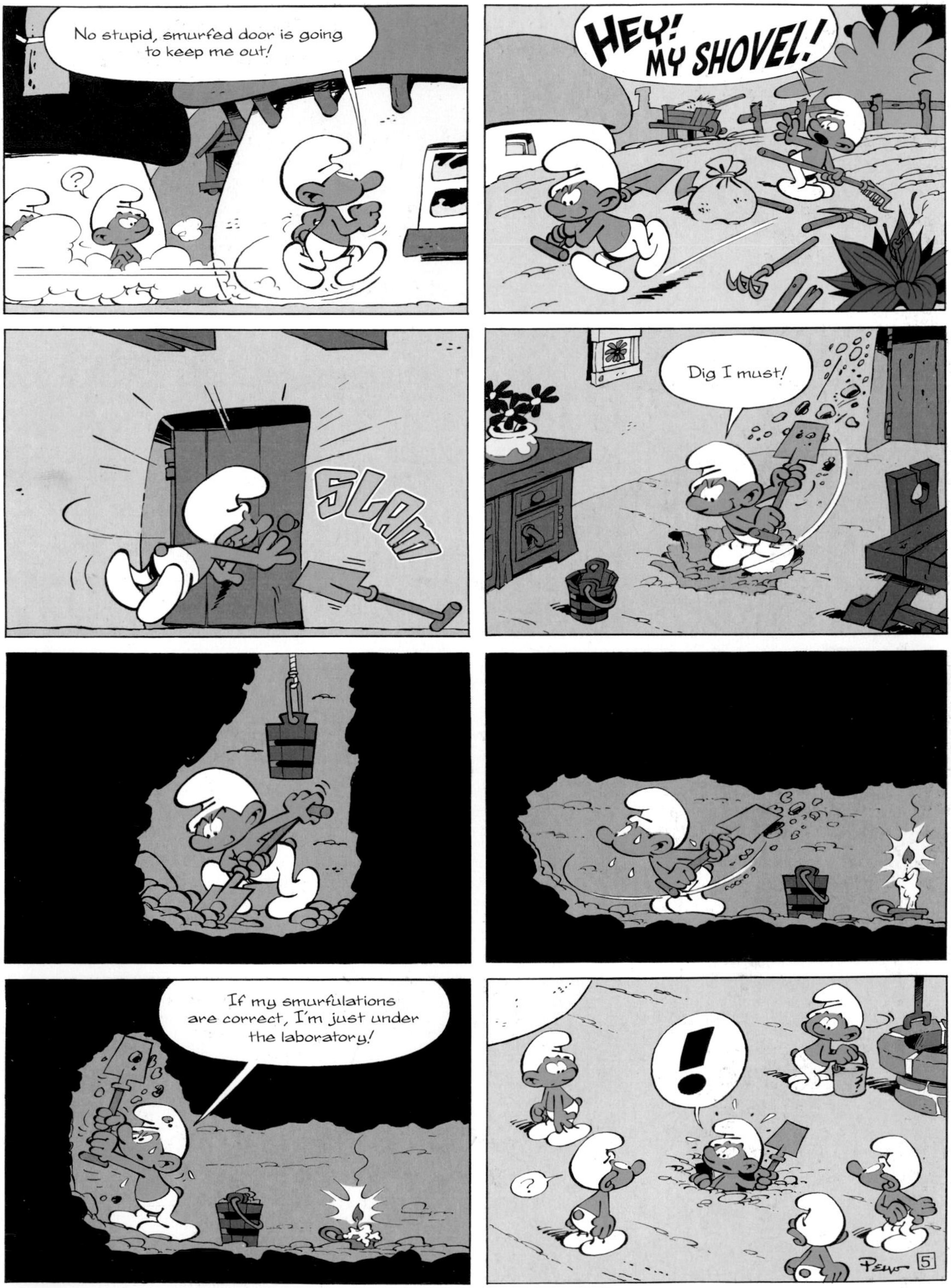
No stupid, smurfed door is going to keep me out!
?
HEY! MY SHOVEL!
SLAM
Dig I must!
If my smurfulations are correct, I'm just under the laboratory!
!
?
Peyo
5

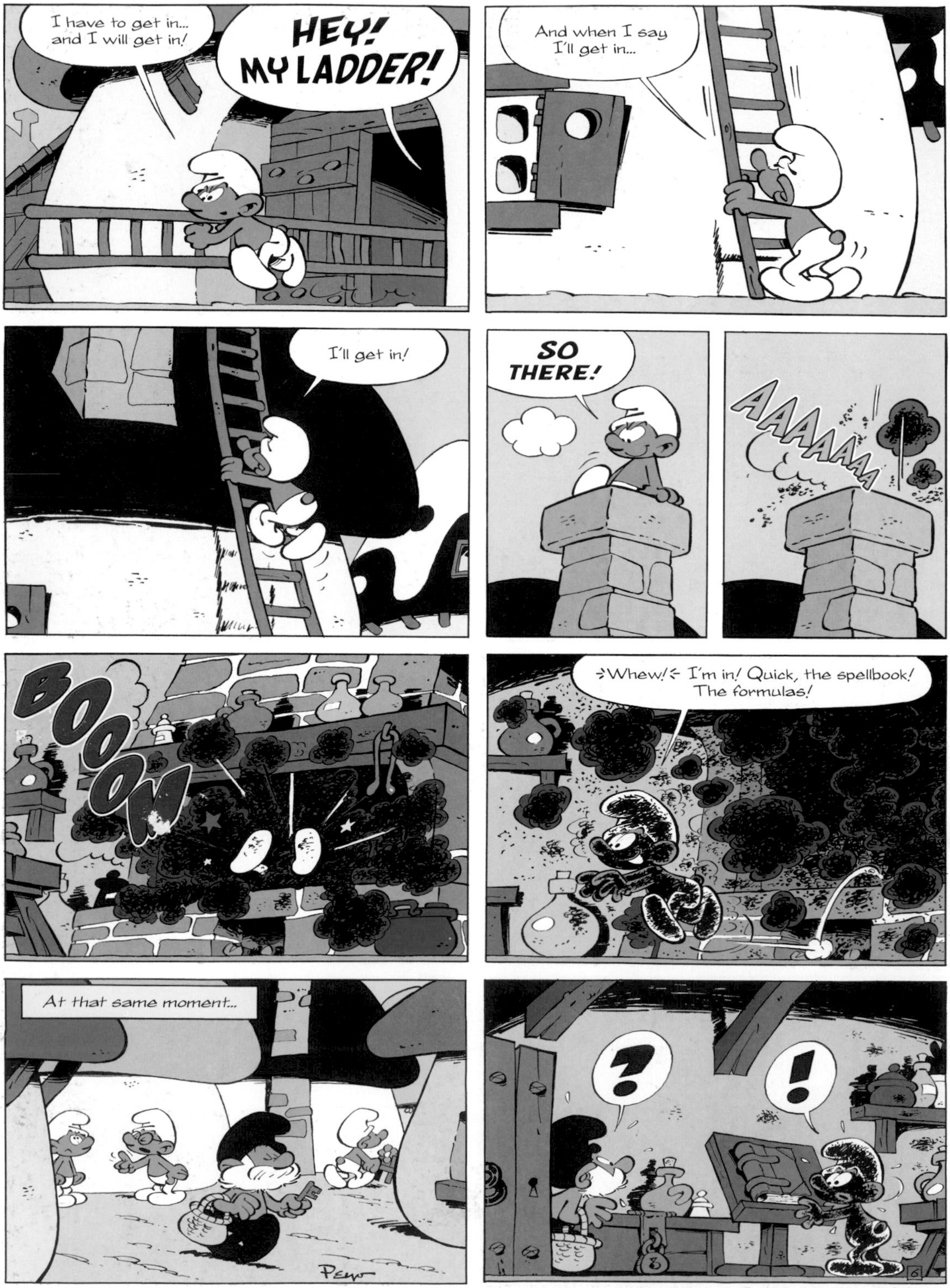
I have to get in... and I will get in!
HEY! MY LADDER!
And when I say I'll get in...
I'll get in!
SO THERE!
AAAAAAA
BOOOOM
Whew! I'm in! Quick, the spellbook! The formulas!
At that same moment...
?
!

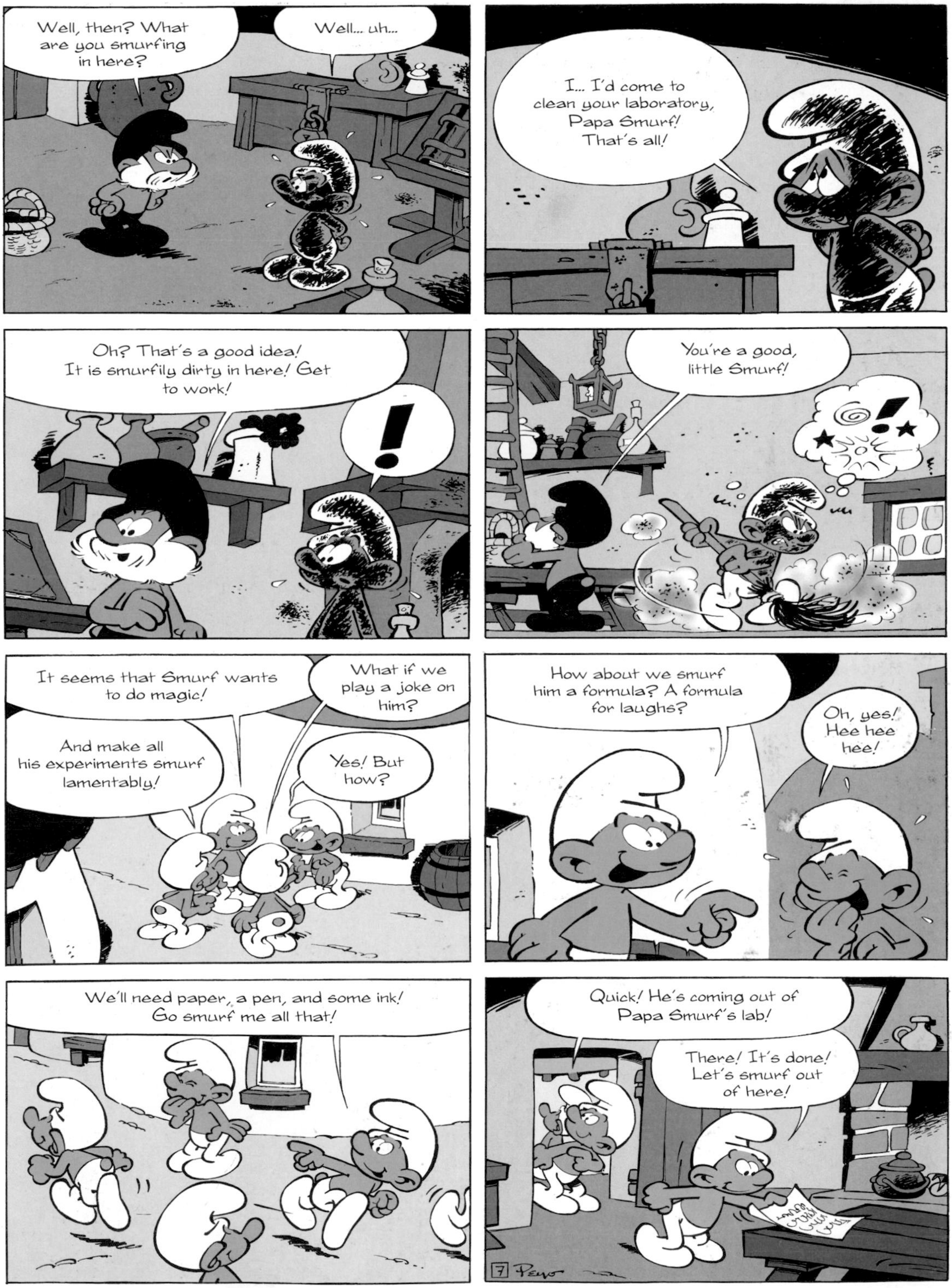
Well, then? What are you smurfing in here?
Well... uh...
I... I'd come to clean your laboratory, Papa Smurf! That's all!
Oh? That's a good idea! It is smurfily dirty in here! Get to work!
!
You're a good, little Smurf!
It seems that Smurf wants to do magic!
What if we play a joke on him?
And make all his experiments smurf lamentably!
Yes! But how?
How about we smurf him a formula? A formula for laughs?
Oh, yes! Hee hee hee!
We'll need paper, a pen, and some ink! Go smurf me all that!
Quick! He's coming out of Papa Smurf's lab!
There! It's done! Let's smurf out of here!

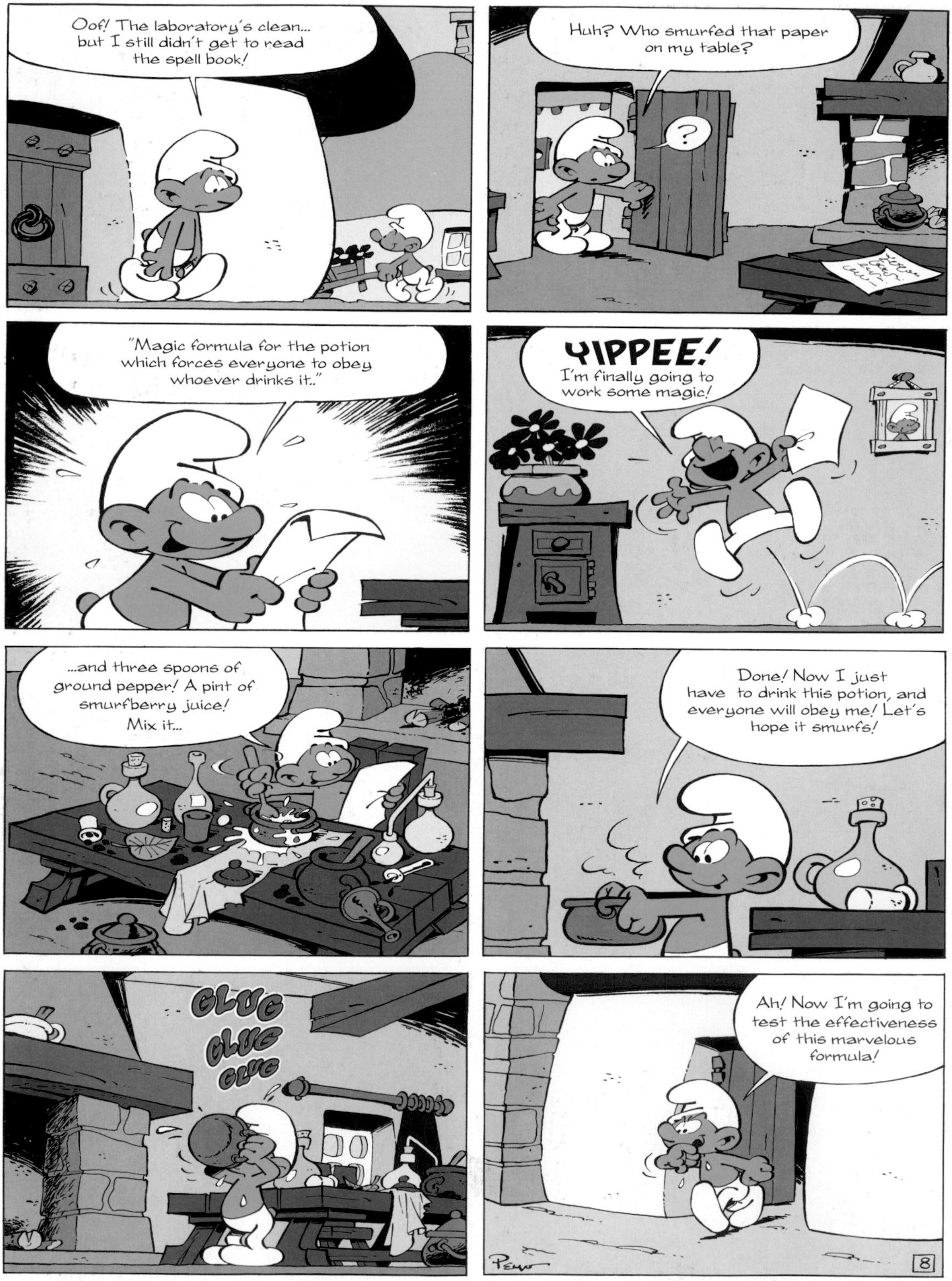
Oof! The laboratory's clean... but I still didn't get to read the spell book!
Huh? Who smurfed that paper on my table?
?
"Magic formula for the potion which forces everyone to obey whoever drinks it.."
YIPPEE!
I'm finally going to work some magic!
...and three spoons of ground pepper! A pint of smurfberry juice! Mix it...
Done! Now I just have to drink this potion, and everyone will obey me! Let's hope it smurfs!
GLUG
GLUG
GLUG
Ah! Now I'm going to test the effectiveness of this marvelous formula!
Peyo
8

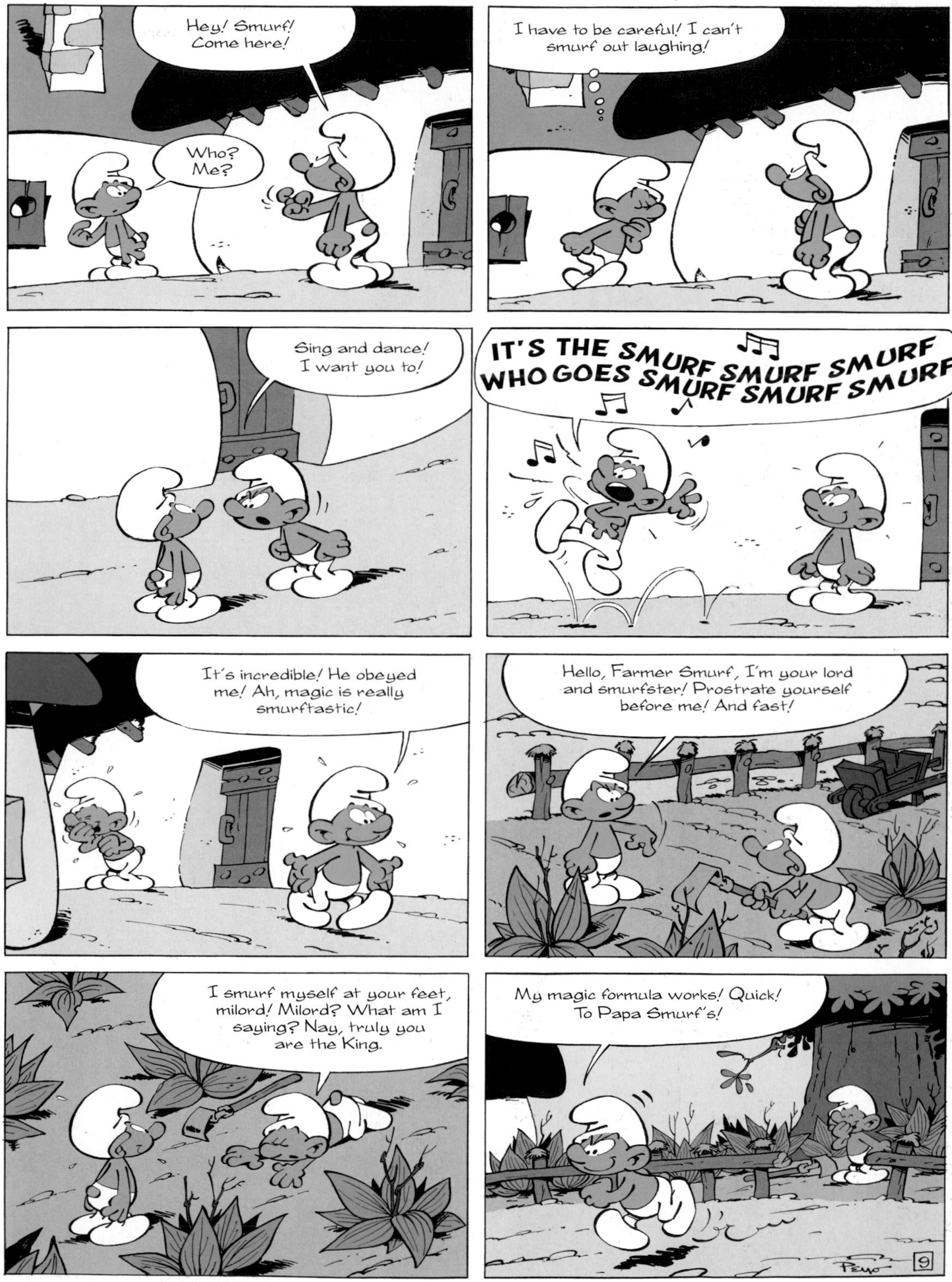
Hey! Smurf! Come here!
Who? Me?
I have to be careful! I can't smurf out laughing!
Sing and dance! I want you to!
IT'S THE SMURF SMURF SMURF WHO GOES SMURF SMURF SMURF
It's incredible! He obeyed me! Ah, magic is really smurftastic!
Hello, Farmer Smurf, I'm your lord and smurfster! Prostrate yourself before me! And fast!
I smurf myself at your feet, milord! Milord? What am I saying? Nay, truly you are the King.
My magic formula works! Quick! To Papa Smurf's!
9
Peyo

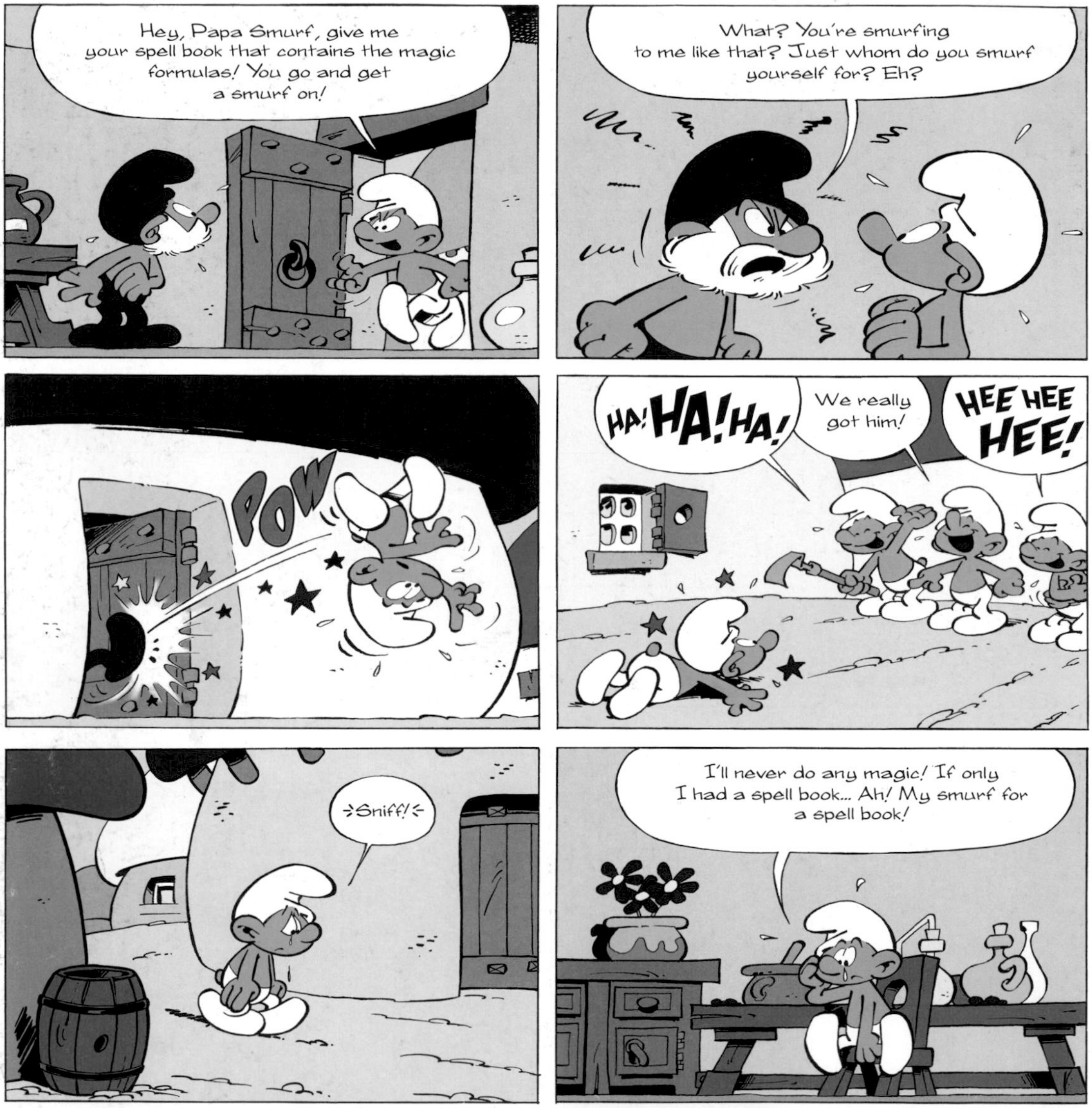
Hey, Papa Smurf, give me your spell book that contains the magic formulas! You go and get a smurf on!
What? You're smurfing to me like that? Just whom do you smurf yourself for? Eh?
POW
HA! HA! HA!
We really got him!
HEE HEE HEE!
Sniff!
I'll never do any magic! If only I had a spell book... Ah! My smurf for a spell book!
Wait... I got it! Gargamel, our enemy, is a sorcerer!
?
I can surely smurf some magic formulas at his home!

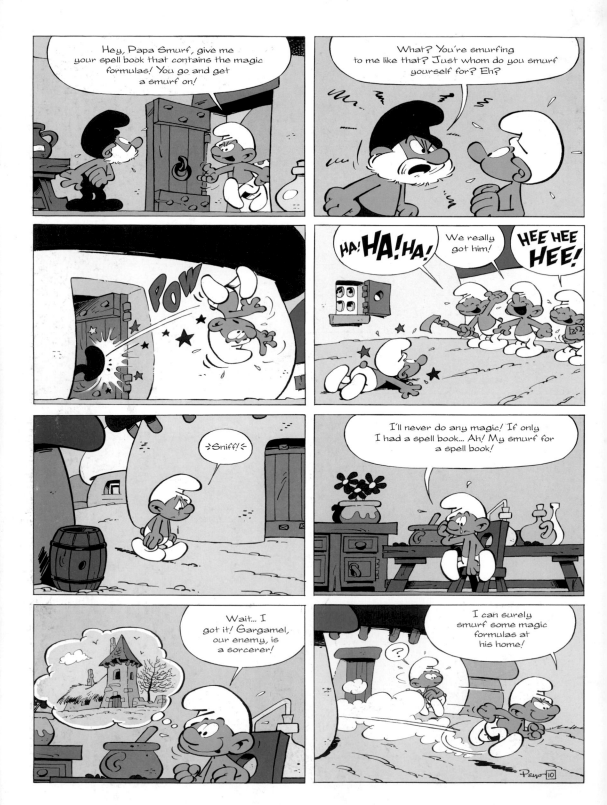

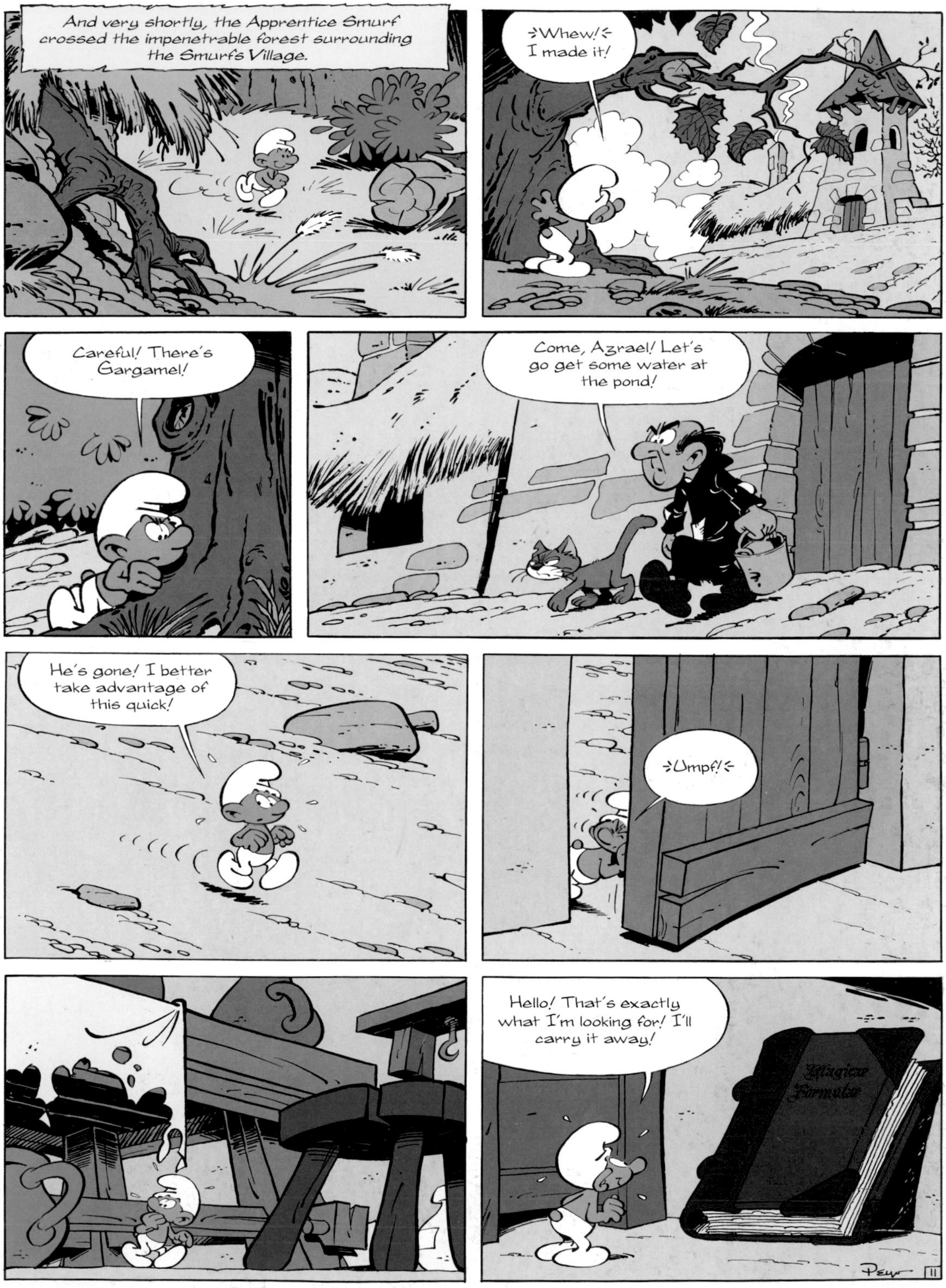

And very shortly, the Apprentice Smurf crossed the impenetrable forest surrounding the Smurfs Village.
Whew! I made it!
Careful! There's Gargamel!
Come, Azrael! Let's go get some water at the pond!
He's gone! I better take advantage of this quick!
Umpf!
Hello! That's exactly what I'm looking for! I'll carry it away!
Magical Formulas
Peyo
11

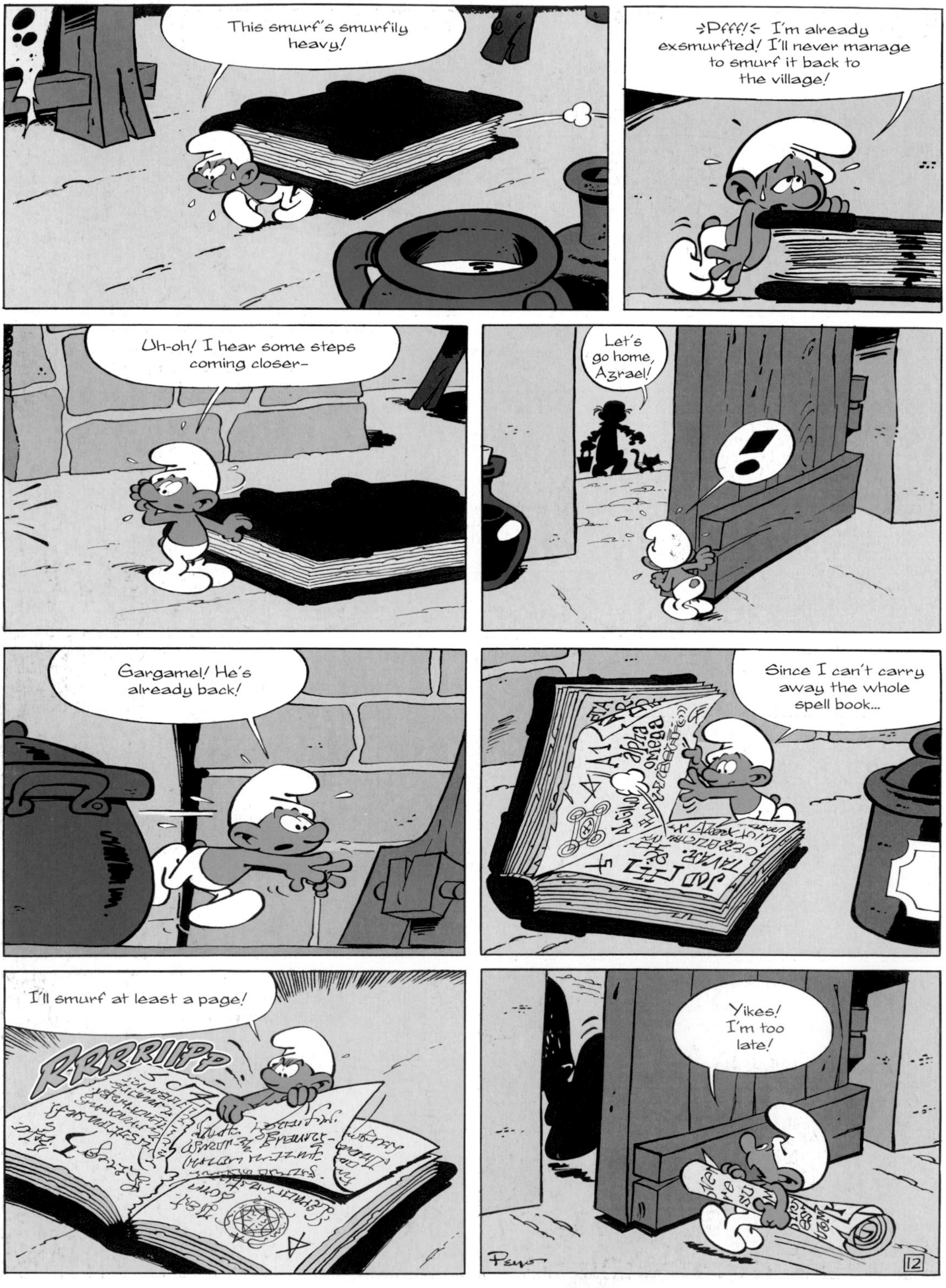
This smurf's smurfily heavy!
-Pfff!- I'm already exsmurfted! I'll never manage to smurf it back to the village!
Uh-oh! I hear some steps coming closer-
Let's go home, Azrael!
!
Gargamel! He's already back!
Since I can't carry away the whole spell book...
I'll smurf at least a page!
RRRRIIPP
Yikes! I'm too late!
Peyo
12

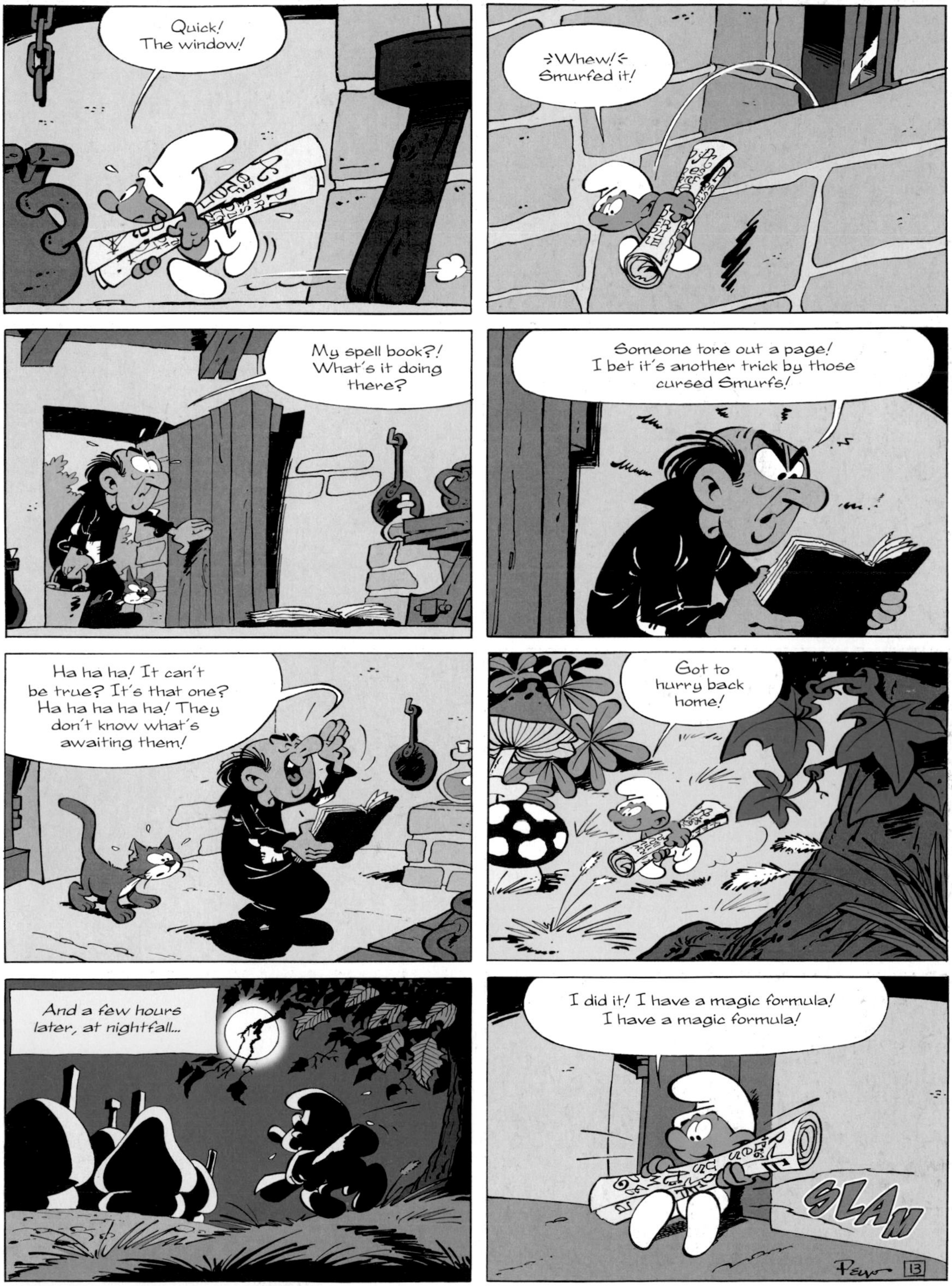
Quick! The window!
Whew! Smurfed it!
My spell book?! What's it doing there?
Someone tore out a page! I bet it's another trick by those cursed Smurfs!
Ha ha ha! It can't be true? It's that one? Ha ha ha ha ha! They don't know what's awaiting them!
Got to hurry back home!
And a few hours later, at nightfall...
I did it! I have a magic formula! I have a magic formula!
SLAM
Peyo
13

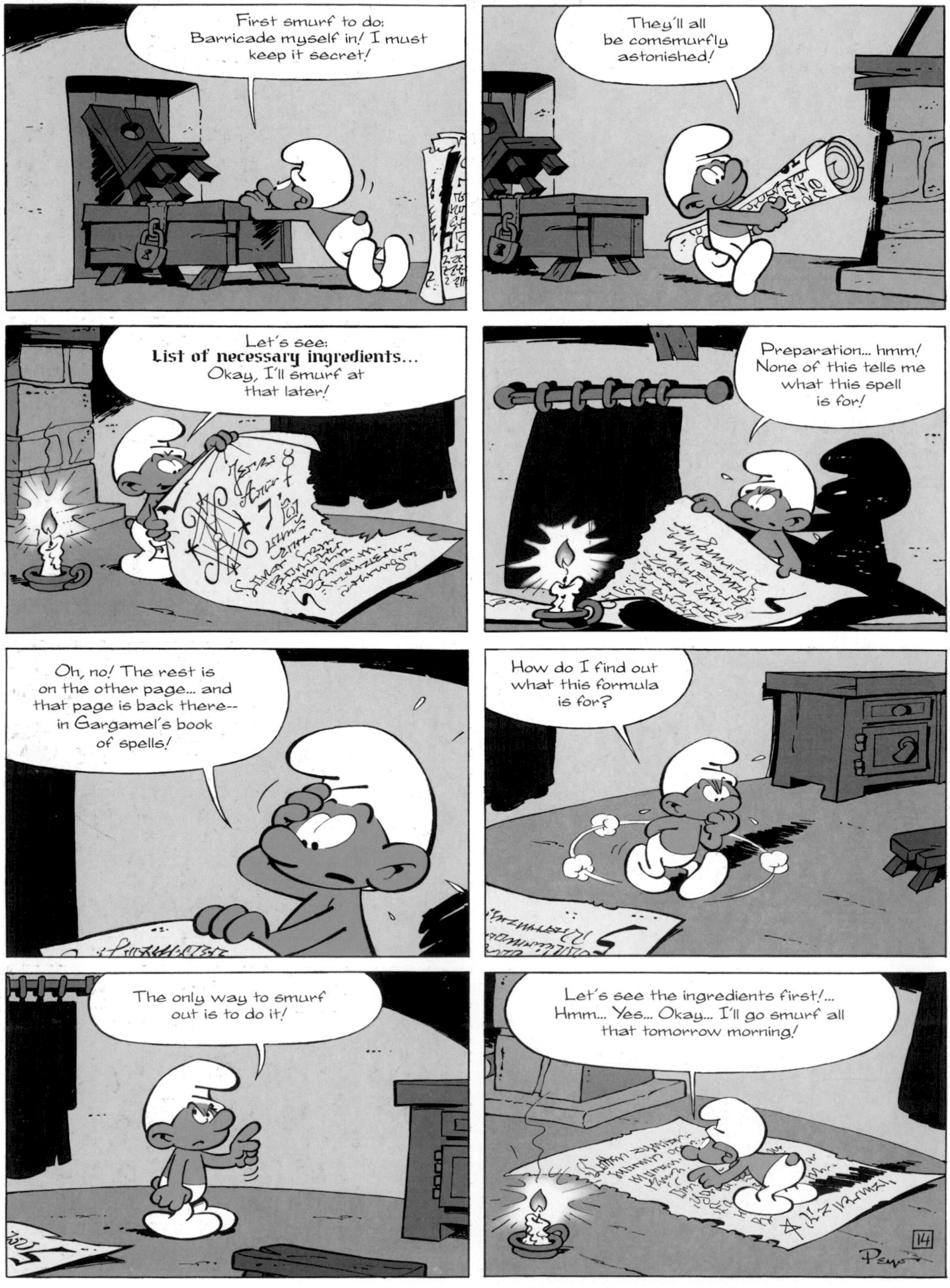

First smurf to do: Barricade myself in! I must keep it secret!
They'll all be comsmurfly astonished!
Let's see: **List of necessary ingredients...** Okay, I'll smurf at that later!
Preparation... hmm! None of this tells me what this spell is for!
Oh, no! The rest is on the other page... and that page is back there-- in Gargamel's book of spells!
How do I find out what this formula is for?
The only way to smurf out is to do it!
Let's see the ingredients first!... Hmm... Yes... Okay... I'll go smurf all that tomorrow morning!
14

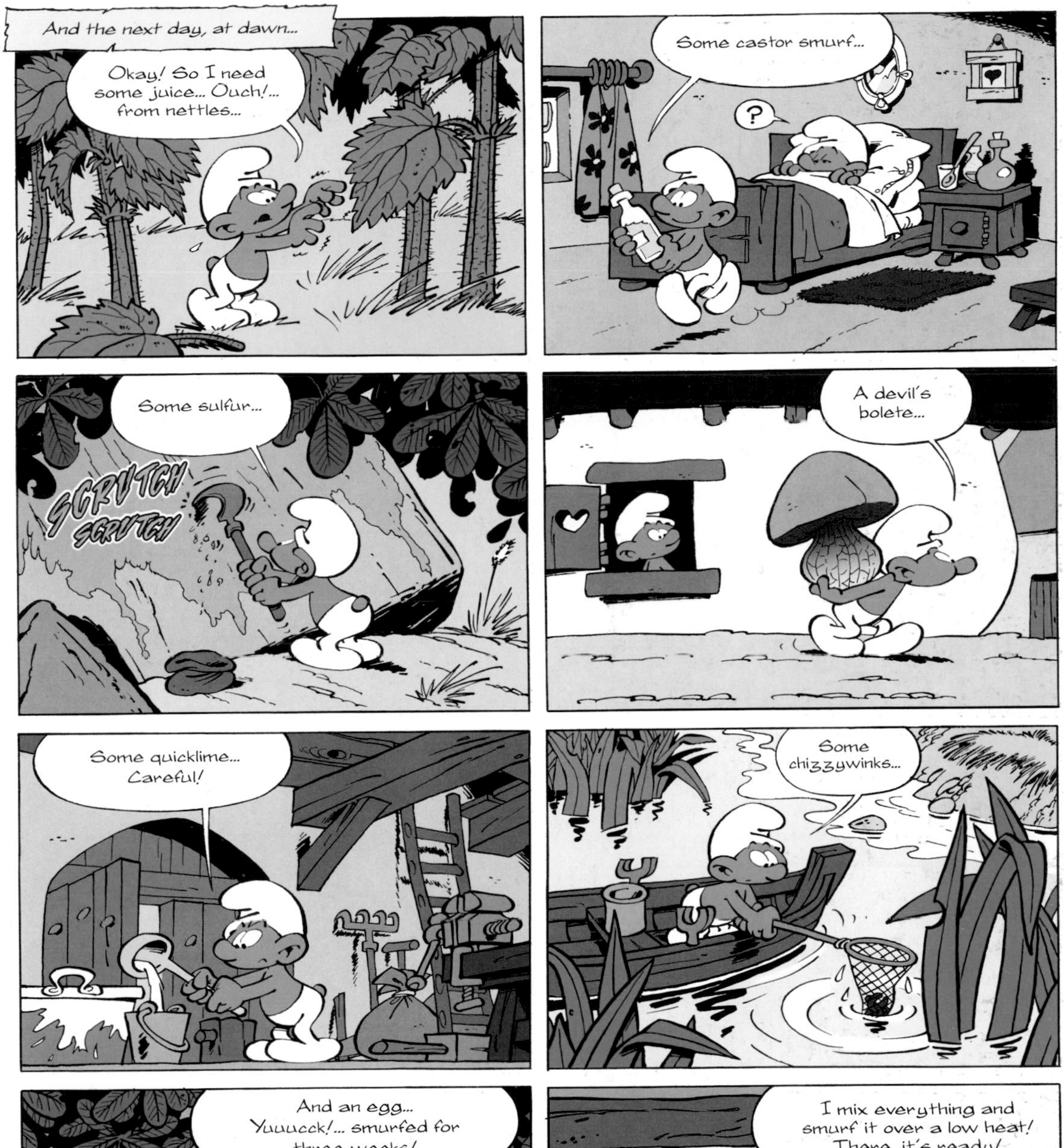
And the next day, at dawn...
Okay! So I need some juice... Ouch!... from nettles...
Some castor smurf...
?
Some sulfur...
SCRUTCH SCRUTCH
A devil's bolete...
Some quicklime... Careful!
Some chizzywinks...
And an egg... Yuuucck!... smurfed for three weeks!
Peyo
I mix everything and smurf it over a low heat! There, it's ready!

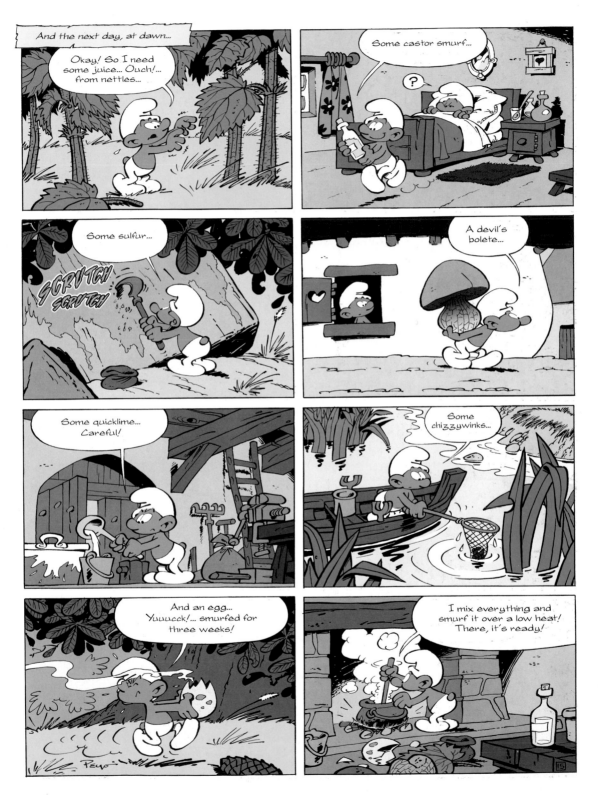

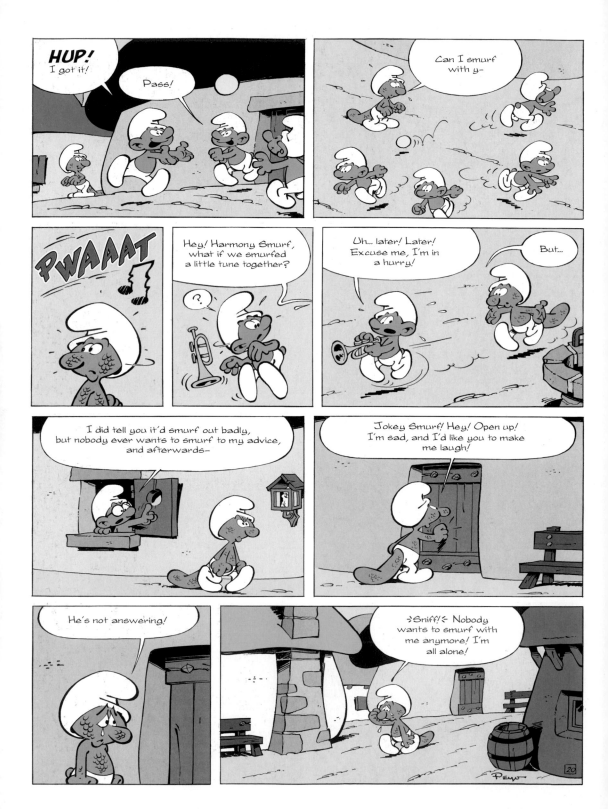

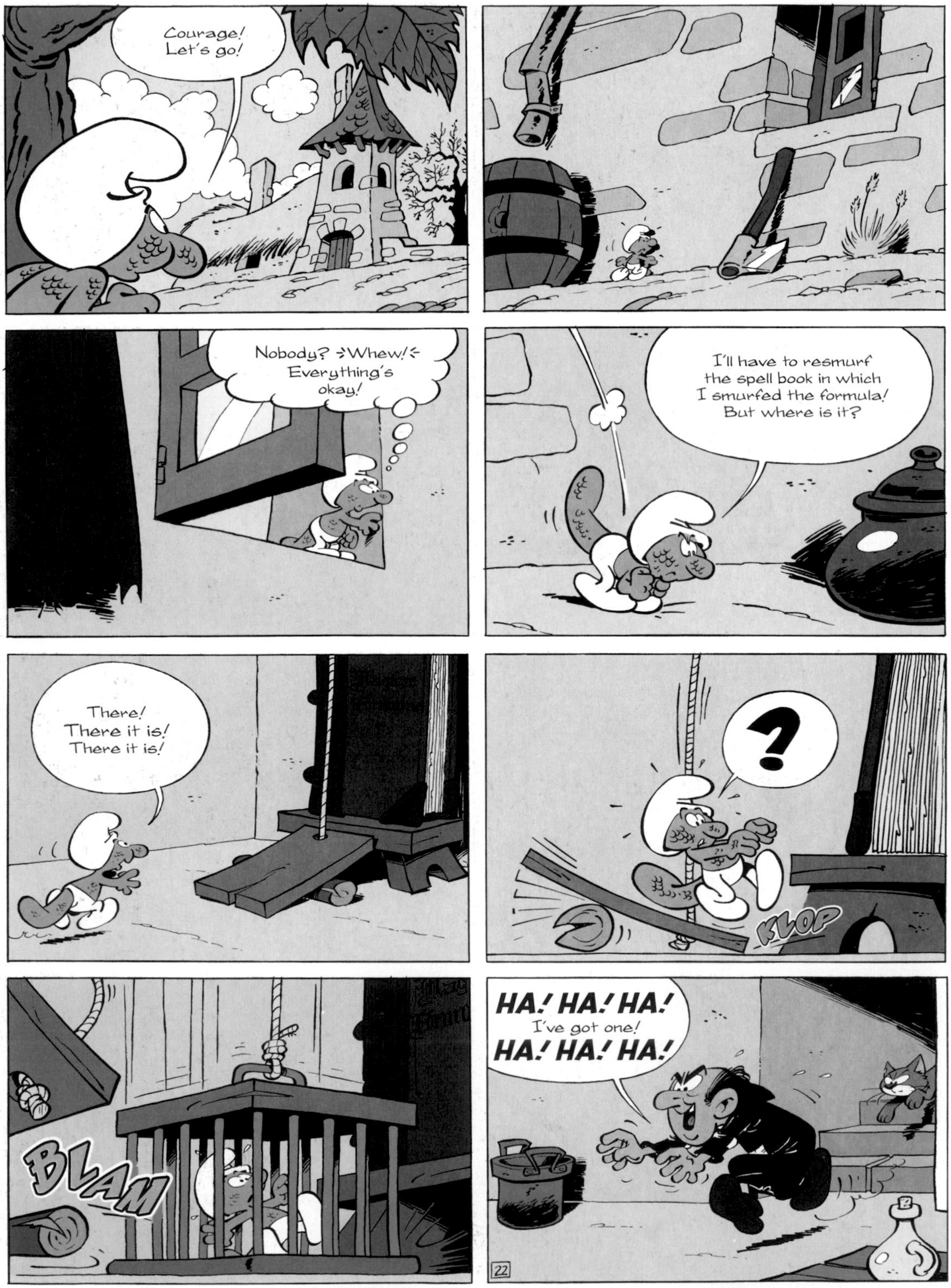

Courage! Let's go!
Nobody? Whew! Everything's okay!
I'll have to resmurf the spell book in which I smurfed the formula! But where is it?
There! There it is! There it is!
?
KLOP
BLAM
HA! HA! HA! I've got one! HA! HA! HA!
22

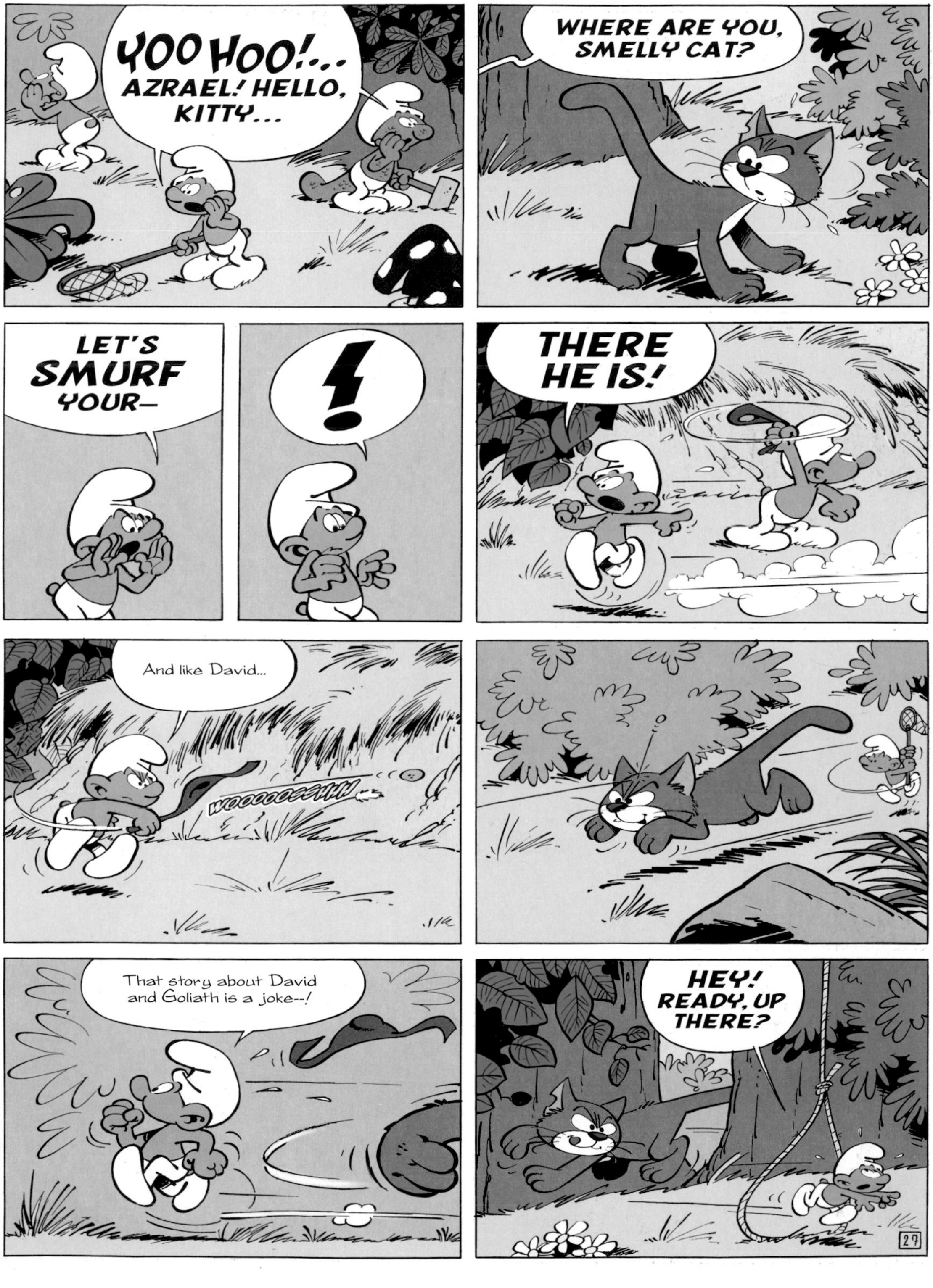
YOO HOO!... AZRAEL! HELLO, KITTY...
WHERE ARE YOU, SMELLY CAT?
LET'S SMURF YOUR—
!
THERE HE IS!
And like David...
WOOOOOSSHHH
That story about David and Goliath is a joke--!
HEY! READY, UP THERE?
27

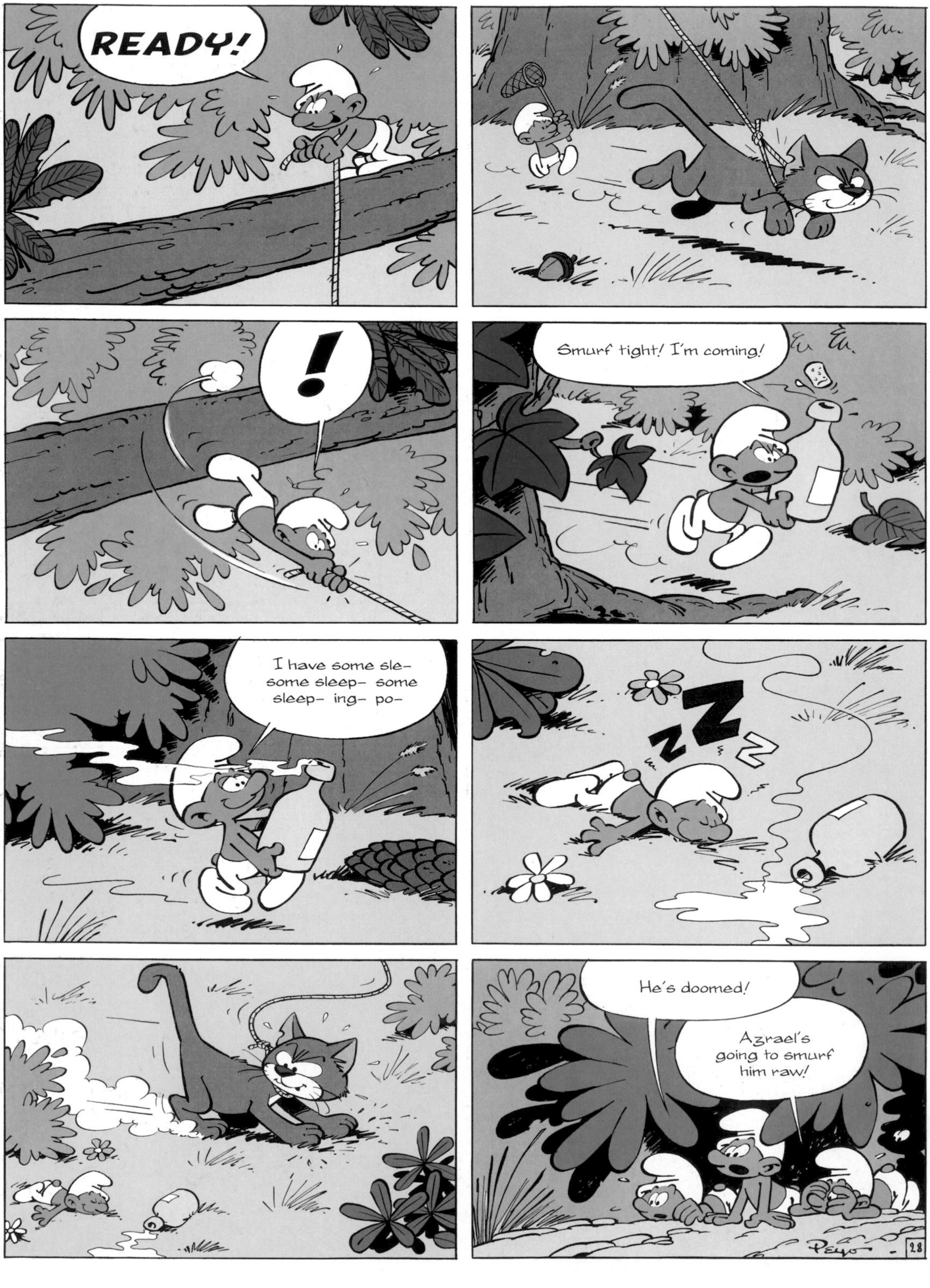
READY!
!
Smurf tight! I'm coming!
I have some sle- some sleep- some sleep- ing- po-
ZZZZ
He's doomed!
Azrael's going to smurf him raw!

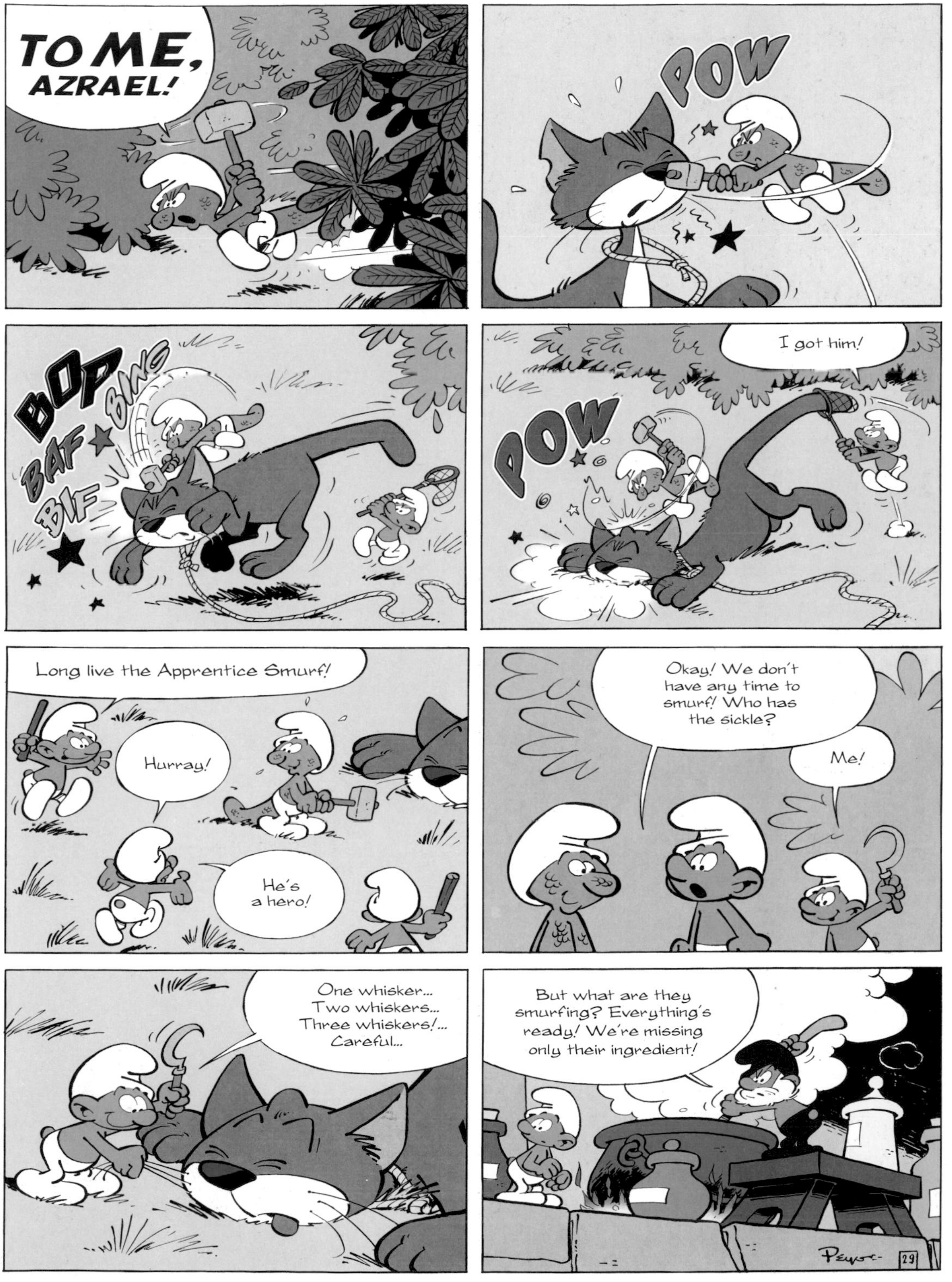
TO ME, AZRAEL!
POW
BOP
BAF
BING
BIF
I got him!
POW
Long live the Apprentice Smurf!
Hurray!
He's a hero!
Okay! We don't have any time to smurf! Who has the sickle?
Me!
One whisker... Two whiskers... Three whiskers!... Careful...
But what are they smurfing? Everything's ready! We're missing only their ingredient!
29

SMURF TRAPS

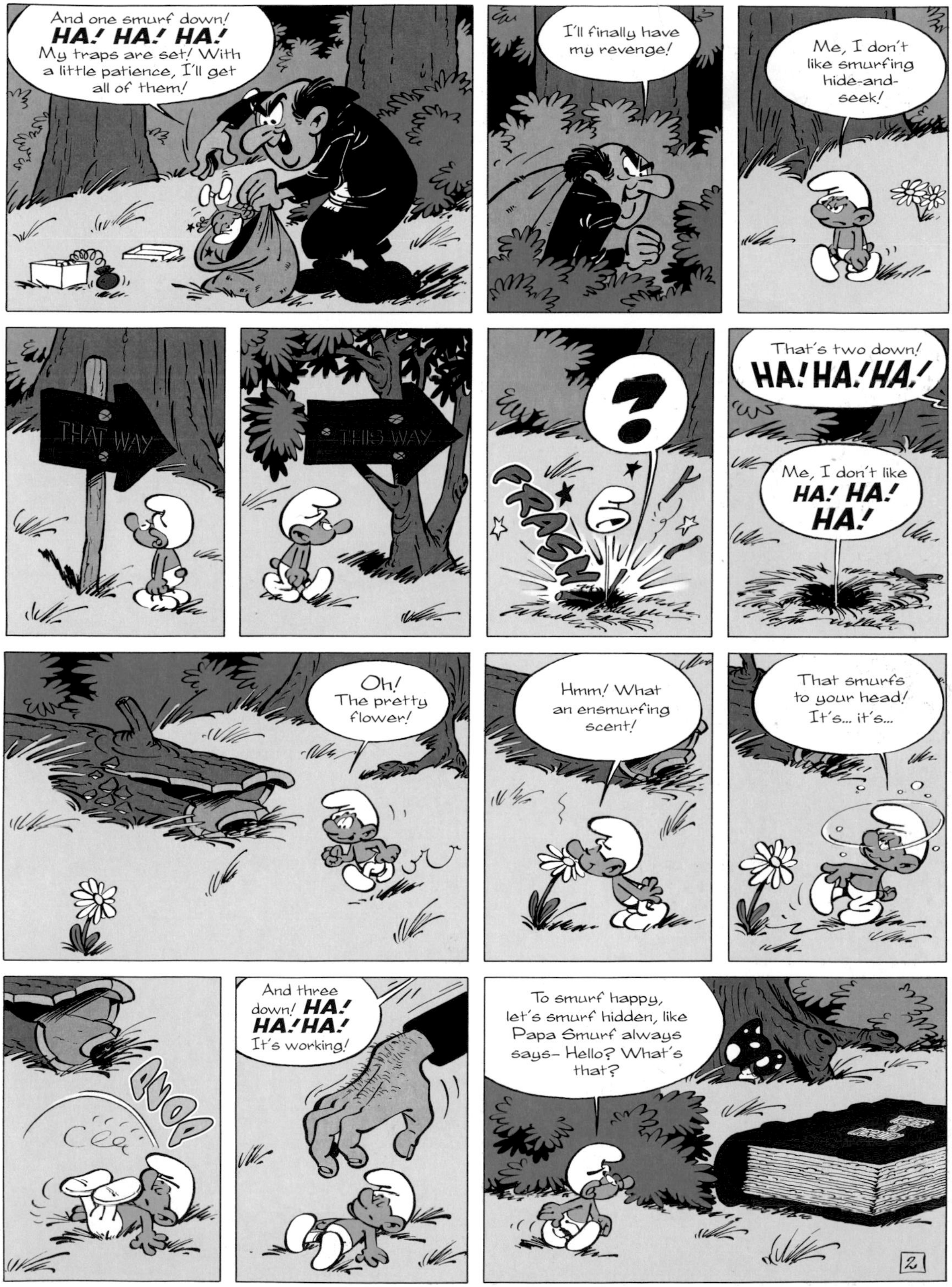
And one smurf down! **HA! HA! HA!** My traps are set! With a little patience, I'll get all of them!
I'll finally have my revenge!
Me, I don't like smurfing hide-and-seek!
THAT WAY
THIS WAY
?
CRASH
That's two down! **HA! HA! HA!**
Me, I don't like **HA! HA! HA!**
Oh! The pretty flower!
Hmm! What an ensmurfing scent!
That smurfs to your head! It's... it's...
And three down! **HA! HA! HA!** It's working!
To smurf happy, let's smurf hidden, like Papa Smurf always says– Hello? What's that?
2

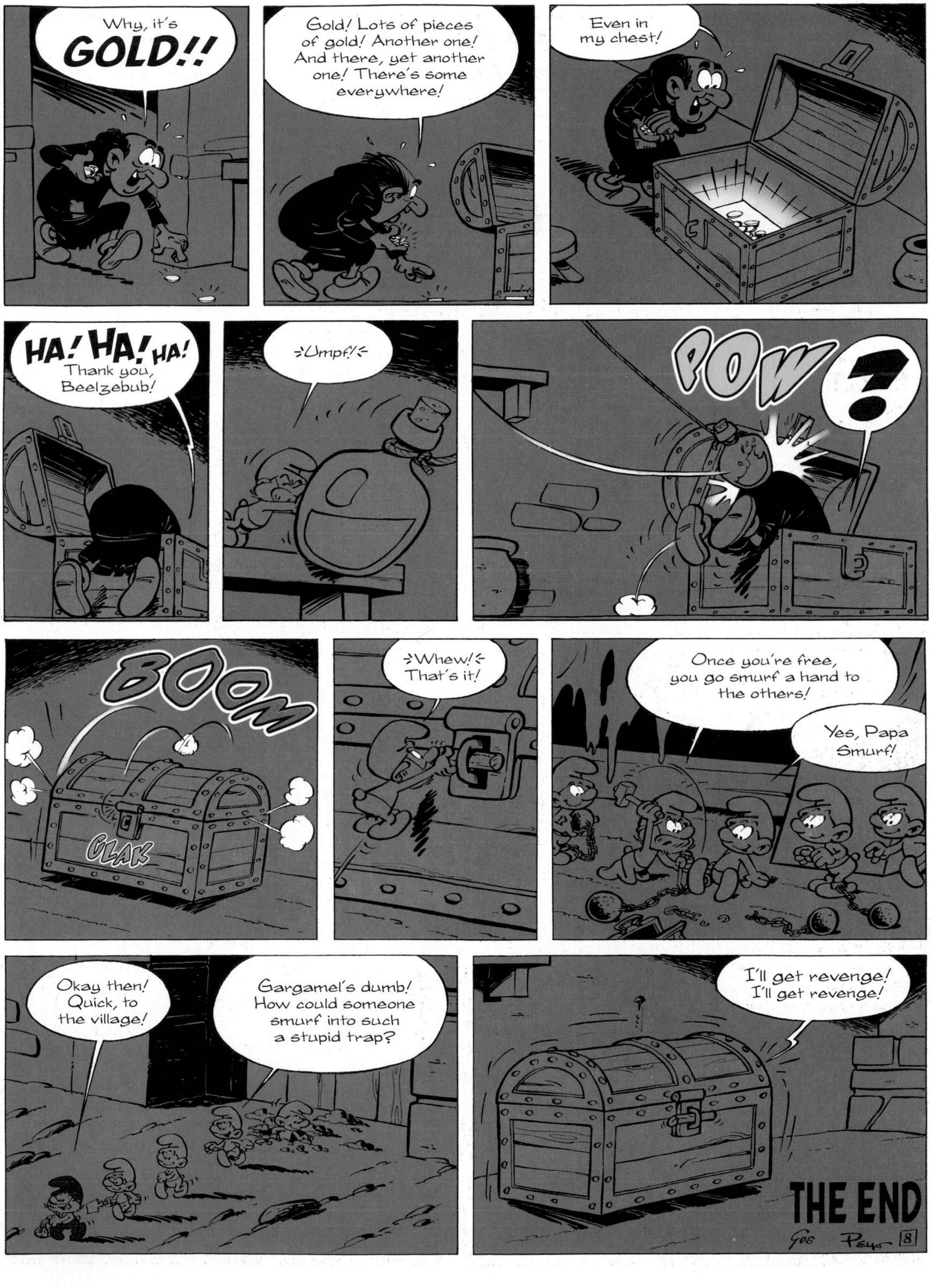
Why, it's GOLD!!
Gold! Lots of pieces of gold! Another one! And there, yet another one! There's some everywhere!
Even in my chest!
HA! HA! HA! Thank you, Beelzebub!
Umpf!
POW
?
BOOM
CLAK
Whew! That's it!
Once you're free, you go smurf a hand to the others!
Yes, Papa Smurf!
Okay then! Quick, to the village!
Gargamel's dumb! How could someone smurf into such a stupid trap?
I'll get revenge! I'll get revenge!
THE END
8

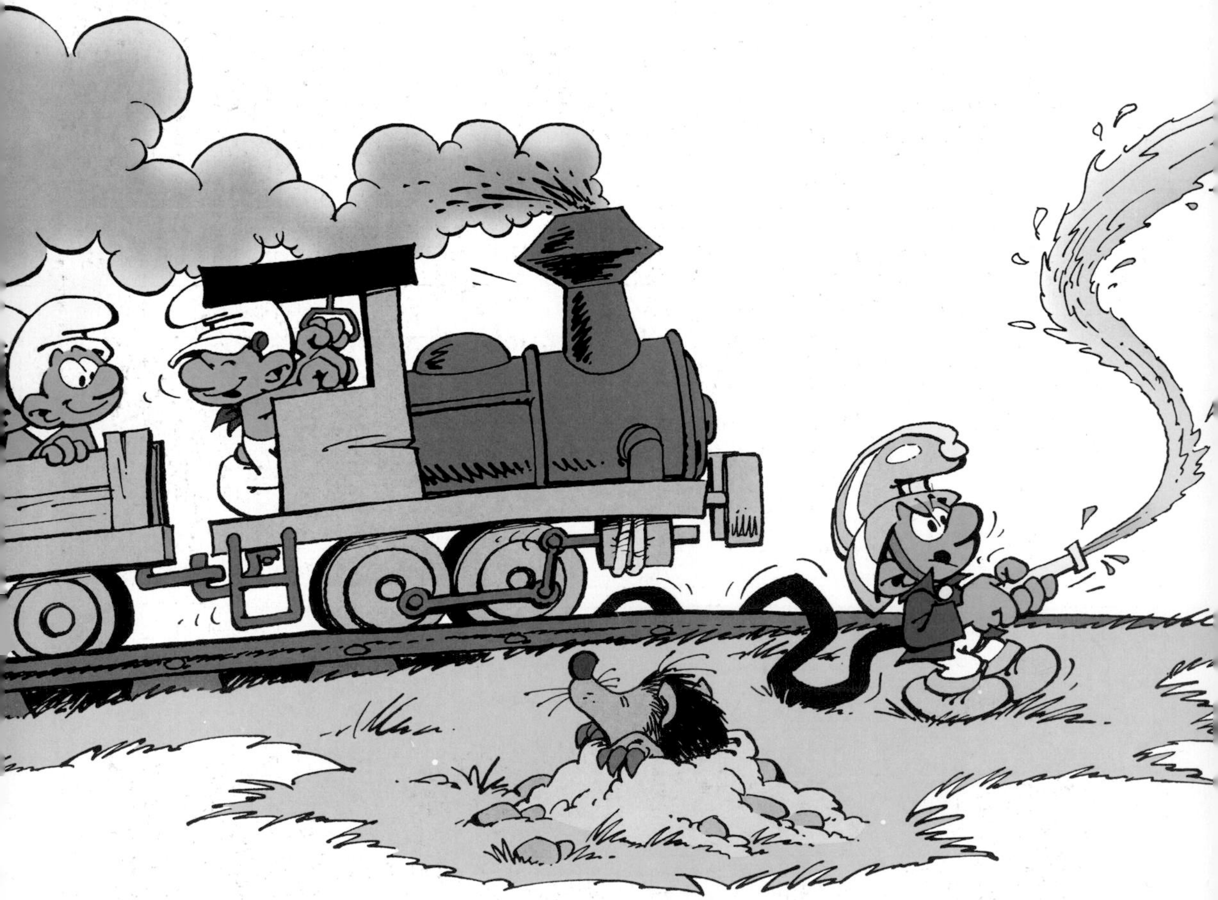

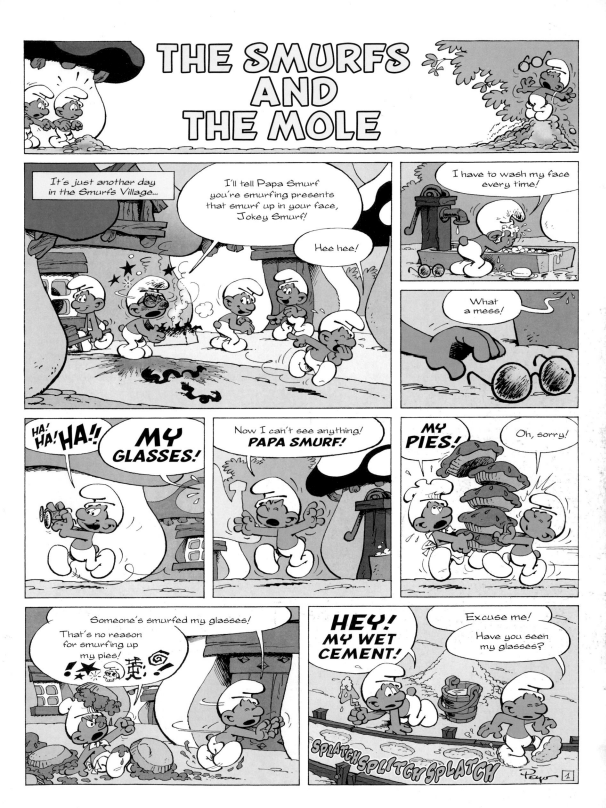

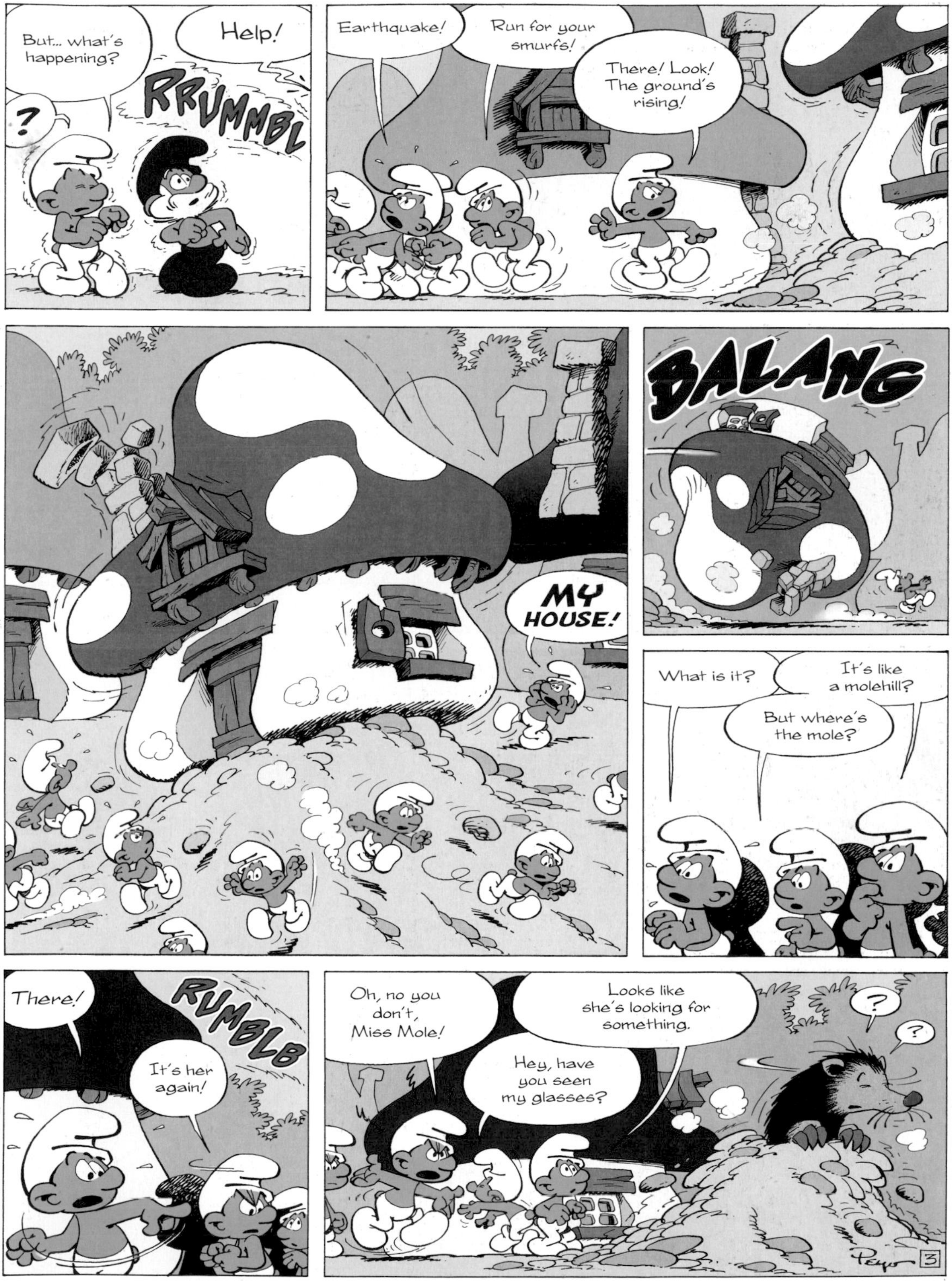
But... what's happening?
Help!
?
RRUMMBL
Earthquake!
Run for your smurfs!
There! Look! The ground's rising!
MY HOUSE!
BALANG
What is it?
It's like a molehill?
But where's the mole?
There!
RUMBLB
It's her again!
Oh, no you don't, Miss Mole!
Looks like she's looking for something.
Hey, have you seen my glasses?
?
?
Peyo
3

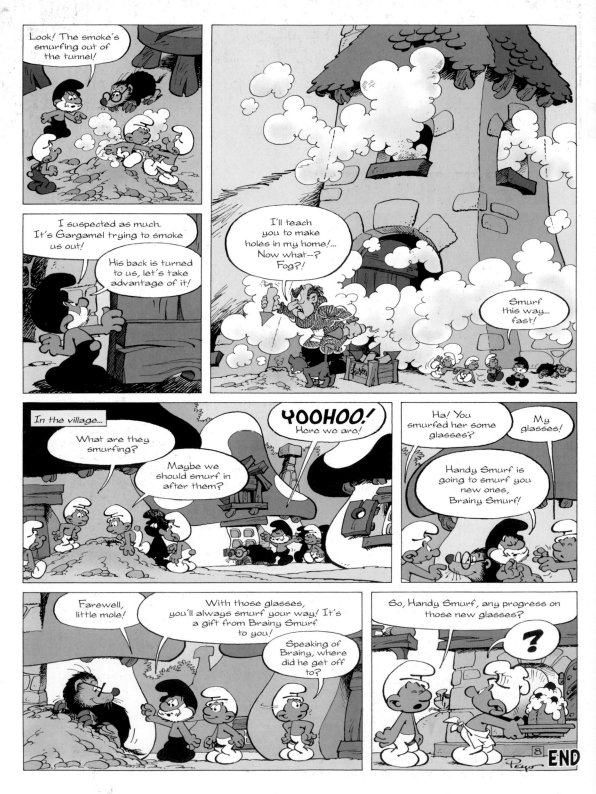

WATCH OUT FOR PAPERCUTZ™

Welcome to the enchanting and educational eighth SMURFS graphic novel from Papercutz, the mild-mannered publishers of great graphic novels for all ages. I'm Jim Salicrup, the apprehensive Smurf-in-Chief, wading his way through Gargamel's Smurf traps to tell you all the latest news from Papercutz. Well, I would if I had more room! But we squeeze in so many Smurfs in every SMURFS graphic novel that all I can do is suggest that you visit www.papercutz.com and check out all the exciting titles we produce, such as CLASSICS ILLUSTRATED, celebrating its big 70th anniversary; DISNEY FAIRIES, featuring Tinker Bell; GARFIELD & Co, based on the hit Cartoon Network TV series; GERONIMO STILTON, who's saving the future, by protecting the past; NANCY DREW, America's favorite Girl Detective; and PAPERCUTZ SLICES, the world's greatest series of parody graphic novels! We're also unleashing a slew of new titles soon, so be sure to keep an eye on our website!

In the meantime, I wanted to tell you about some of the folks responsible for bringing you these amazing SMURFS graphic novels. Obviously, the most important person of all is Peyo! Without him the world would be Smurfless— what a terrible thought! You can learn all about the creator of THE SMURFS in Matt. Murray's "The World of Smurfs: A Celebration of Tiny Blue Proportions," the book no true Smurfs-fan should be without. But let me tell you about some of the other folks who help produce the Papercutz editions. You might say it takes a village, a Smurfs Village, to assemble each SMURFS graphic novel. One such person is the award-winning designer Adam Grano.

There's an interesting story about how Adam got the assignment of Smurfic Designer. When he heard that Papercutz publisher Terry Nantier had acquired the North American publishing rights to THE SMURFS, Adam knew he had to do something special to get Terry's attention to make his pitch. After all, Adam lives about

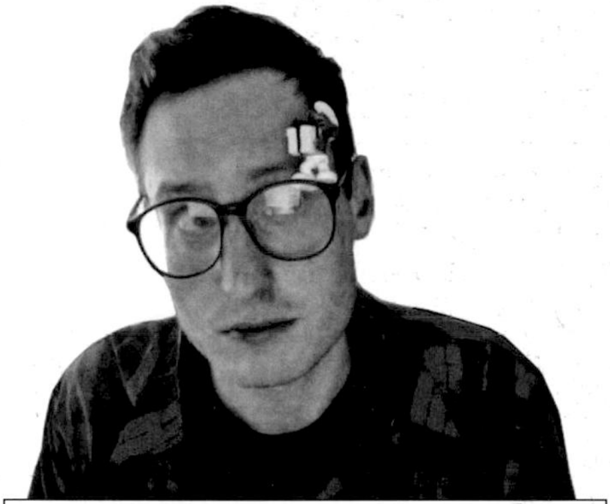

Smurfic Designer Adam Grano (and Jokey Smurf)

3,000 miles west from the palatial Papercutz offices. Adam posted a plea to Terry online at The Comics Journal website, a very popular site for serious comic art afficianados. Adam wrote, "...I'd like to make a public appeal to you to allow me to design [the] upcoming SMURFS books. If I'm too late with this appeal, then ... bummer, but I just heard about your project yesterday... If it helps, I would happily work for a pittance — this is the comics industry after all." Adam sure knows how to appeal to a publisher's heart... and purse! But what really sold us, aside from his incredible talent, was when Adam wrote...

"I just kinda love the Smurfs.

"That feels strange to say, but I really do have a soft spot for the little blue halflings. I grew up on them." Well, talk about an offer you can't refuse... ! Naturally, we contacted Adam and signed him up, and have been thrilled with the Smurftastic results!

We'll talk about more behind-the-scenes folks in the next "Watch Out for Papercutz" column in THE SMURFS #9 "Gargamel and the Smurfs," coming November 2011! See you then!

Jim

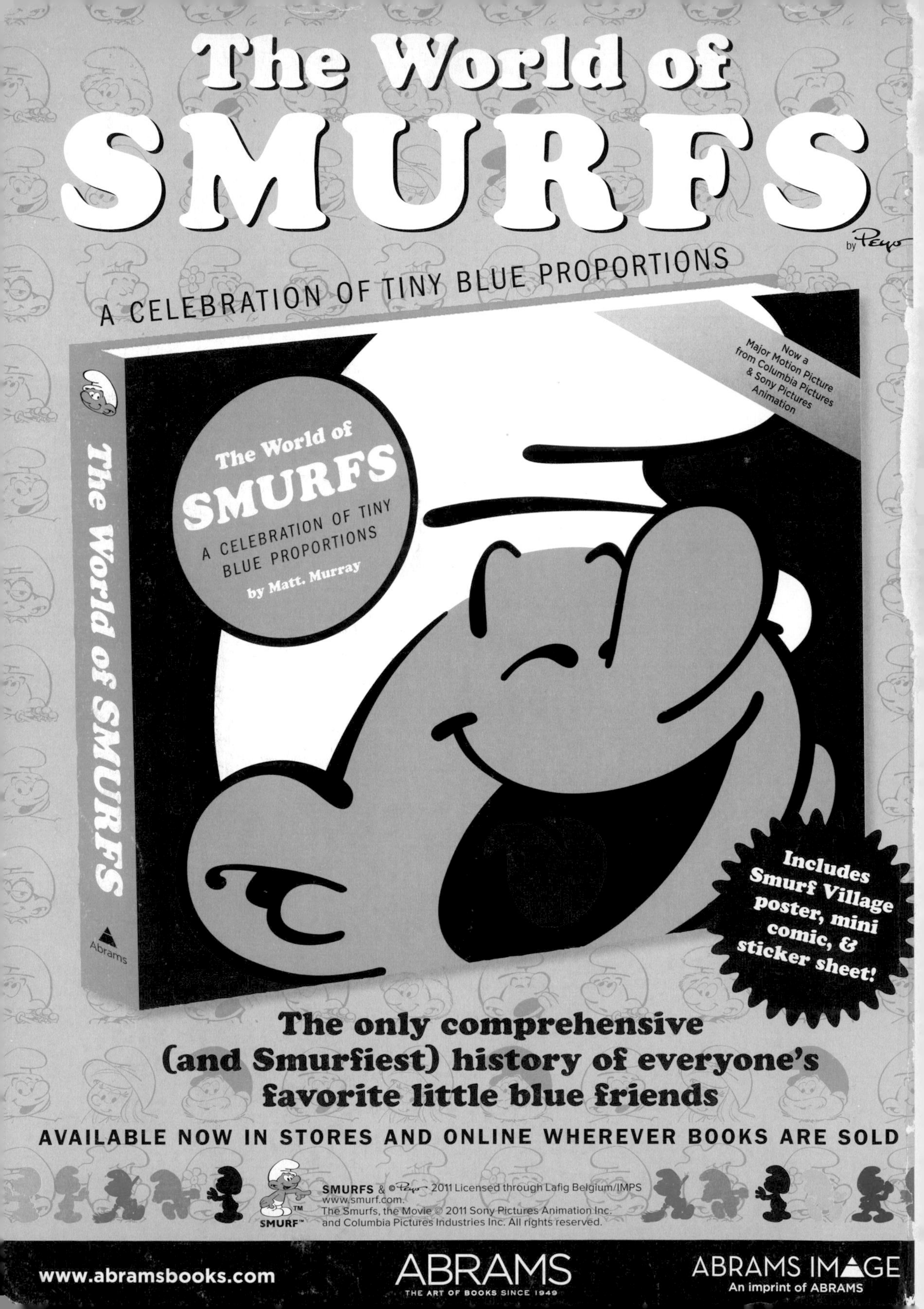

The World of
SMURFS
by Peyo
A CELEBRATION OF TINY BLUE PROPORTIONS
Now a Major Motion Picture from Columbia Pictures & Sony Pictures Animation
The World of SMURFS
A CELEBRATION OF TINY BLUE PROPORTIONS
by Matt. Murray
The World of SMURFS
Abrams
Includes Smurf Village poster, mini comic, & sticker sheet!
The only comprehensive (and Smurfiest) history of everyone's favorite little blue friends
AVAILABLE NOW IN STORES AND ONLINE WHEREVER BOOKS ARE SOLD
SMURF™
SMURFS & © Peyo 2011 Licensed through Lafig Belgium/IMPS www.smurf.com.
The Smurfs, the Movie © 2011 Sony Pictures Animation Inc. and Columbia Pictures Industries Inc. All rights reserved.
www.abramsbooks.com
ABRAMS
THE ART OF BOOKS SINCE 1949
ABRAMS IMAGE
An imprint of ABRAMS